Titles Also By G.R. Ording

Operation North Star
Smile Of The Tiger
Night Of The Lotus Lanterns
Criss-Cross
The Omega Solution
Command Target
In The Shadow Of The Fox
Point Zero
The Churchill Equation

HIGH TIDE

G.R. Ording

BookLocker

FOREWORD

Operation Tiger, was the code name for one in a series of large-scale rehearsals for the D-Day invasion of Normandy, which took place in April 1944 on Slapton Sands in Devon. Coordination and communication problems resulted in friendly fire deaths during the exercise, and an Allied convoy positioning itself for the landing was attacked by E-boats of Germany's Krigsmarine, resulting in the deaths of at least 749 American servicemen. Because of the impending invasion of Normandy, the incident was under the strictest secrecy.

1

He was lifted on the crest of a wave; he saw what was left of the LST, her bow already under water. There were bodies all around, clear in the early morning light. Far beyond, the sea was on fire with burning oil, then there was an explosion, the stern of the LST lifted and then was gone.

He skidded down the other side of the wave, buoyant in his lifejacket, and then another wave washed over him and he choked as he struggled for breath, aware of the intense pain from a wound to the right side of his head and an equal amount of pain in his left foot.

The sea was running very fast, it seemed to take hold of him, carrying him along at an incredible rate, the cries of men faded into the mist and fog. Again he was lifted high on a wave, paused for a moment, then swept down very fast and crashed into a large rubber life-raft, the kind found on most ships. He grabbed one of the rope handles and hauled himself into the raft landing on his face. He sat up and looked around for any men in the water, but there were none. The cries were no more, long gone in the early morning light.

He found the first aid kit stored in an inner compartment. There is an open wound to the right side of his head. Blood moved down his face in a steady flow. He took several flat dressing materials and placed it to his wound with one hand and wrapped gauze dressing around with the other hand the best he could. He reached down to check his ankle, it hurt to touch. He felt dizzy and sick, threw up what was most likely seawater. He took to a corner of the raft and darkness came over him suddenly.

In late 1943, as part of the build-up to D-Day, the British government set up a training ground at Slapton Sands, Devon, to be used by Force 'U', the American forces tasked with landing on Omaha and Utah Beach. Slapton Beach was selected for its similarity to both of these beaches.

Four sites were considered for the landings: Brittany, the Cortentin Peninsula, Normandy, and the Pas de Calais. As Brittany and Cotentin are peninsulas, it would have been possible for the Germans to cut off Allied advance at a relatively narrow isthmus, so these sites were rejected.

With the Pas de Calais begin the closest point in continental Europe to Britain, the Germans considered it to be the most likely initial landing zone, so it was the most heavily fortified region. But it offered few opportunities for expansion, as the area is bounded by numerous rivers and canals, whereas landings on a broad front in Normandy was hence chosen as the landing site. This led to the exercises because of the similarly of the sites.

Landing exercises started in December 1943. Exercise Tiger was one of the larger exercises that took place in April 1944. The exercise was to last from 22 April until 30 April 1944, and covered all aspects of the invasion, culminating in a beach landing at Slapton Sands. On board nine large tank landing ships (LSTs), the 30,000 troops prepared for their mock landing, which also included a live-firing exercise.

Protection for the exercise area came from the Royal Navy. Two destroyers, three Motor Torpedo Boats and two Motor Gun Boats patrolled the entrance to Lyme Bay.

The first phase of the exercise focused on marshalling and embarkation drills, and lasted from 22 to 25 April. On the evening of 26 April the first wave of assault troops boarded their transports and set off,

9

the plan being to simulate the Channel crossing by taking a roundabout route through Lyme Bay, in order to arrive off Slapton at first light on 27 April.

The first practice assault took place on the morning of 27 April and was marred by an incident involving friendly fire. H-hour was set for 06:30, and was to include live ammunition to acclimatize the troops to the sights, sounds and even smells of a naval bombardment. During the landing itself, live rounds were to be fired over the heads of the incoming troops by forces on land, for the same reason. This followed an order made by General Dwight D. Eisenhower, the Supreme Allied Commander, who felt that the men must be hardened by exposure to real battle conditions. The exercise was to include naval bombardment by ships fifty minutes prior to the landing.

Several of the landing ships for that morning were delayed and the officer in charge, American Admiral Don P. Moon, decided to delay H-hour for 60 minutes, until 07:30. Some of the landing craft did not receive word of the change. Landing on the beach at their original scheduled time with the high tide, the second wave came under fire suffering an unknown number of casualties.

On the day after the first practice assaults, early on the morning of 28 April, the exercise was blighted when Convoy T-4, consisting of eight LSTs carrying vehicles and combat engineers of the 1st Engineer Special Brigade commanded by Lieutenant Colonel Henry Walker, was attacked by nine German E-boats under the command of Korvettenkapitan Bernd Klug, in Lyme Bay.

Of the two ships assigned to protect the convoy, only one was present. HMS Azalea, a corvette was leading the LSTs in a straight line, a formation that later drew criticism since it presented an easy target to the E-boats. The second ship that was supposed to be present, HMS Scimitar, a World War I destroyer, had been in collision with an LST, suffered structural damage and left the convoy to be repaired at Plymouth. Because the LSTs and British naval headquarters were operating on different frequencies, the American forces did not know this.

HMS Saladin was dispatched as a replacement, but did not arrive in time to help protect the convoy.

The E-boats had left Cherbourg on patrol the previous evening and spotted the convoy early in the morning and attacked.

The ships and their escorts fired back and the E-boats made no more attacks after their initial run. In total 749 servicemen were killed during operation Tiger. Many drowned or died of hypothermia in the cold sea while waiting to be rescued. Many were not shown how to put on their lifebelt correctly, and placed it around their waist, the only available spot because of their large backpacks. In some cases this meant that when they jumped into the water the weight of their combat packs flipped them upside down, dragging their heads underwater and drowning them.

As a result of official embarrassment and concerns over possible leaks just prior to the real invasion, all survivors were sworn to secrecy by their superiors. Ten missing officers involved in the exercise had BIGOT-level clearance for D-day, meaning that they knew the invasion plans and could have compromised the invasion should they have been captured alive. Nine of the men had been found, all dead, except for one unaccounted for, Lieutenant Colonel Henry Walker who had been aboard LST-507, the one he watched sink, and was now adrift in the Channel, but this was unknown to his superiors who believed him to be dead, his body not found.

At Supreme Headquarters Allied Expeditionary Force, General Dwight D. Eisenhower, supreme allied commander, was pacing back and forth smoking a cigarette when Captain John Abe came in with a worried look on his face. Eisenhower turned to face Abe, "What's the damage captain?"

Abe had been the first to report to Eisenhower about the Operation Tiger disaster but did not have all the details. Eisenhower put him in charge to review what had happened and also to recover the dead and wounded.

"I'm afraid it's bad General. We have recovered most of all the dead, 749 total and only a few wounded. A total disaster sir."

"What about the BIGOT's? Where do we stand with them?"

"There were a total of ten BIGOT's in the exercise sir, we have recovered nine."

"Then there is one still missing? Any chance that he is still alive?" Eisenhower asked, lighting another cigarette.

"No sir, we don't believe he survived. We may find his body but more than likely he will never be found."

"I see, and who is it that is missing?"

A Lieutenant Colonel Henry Walker commanding the 1st Engineer Special Brigade. He was aboard LST 507 which is believed to have sunk with all hands."

"Then we can assume that he went down with the vessel?"

"Yes sir, we believe that to be true. We have classified him as deceased, body not recovered. We have searched for two days now and will continue for another two days before we make it official. Searching the area has become difficult because of increased German naval activity, especially the E-boats."

Eisenhower lights a cigarette, "I can see how that would be a problem. Let us hope he went down with the ship. I would hate to think one of our BIGOT's survived and is captured by the enemy since he knows the plans for Operation Overlord and true landing site for the invasion. That would present a big problem. I never did agree with having that many officers who knew of the landing plans and location but I suppose it was necessary."

"I don't believe we have anything to worry about general."

"I hope you are right captain. How did they ever come up with the code name BIGOT anyway?"

"From what I understand it's an acronym for British Invasion of German Occupied Territory.

Someone on General Montgomery's staff came up with it. There is a story that some junior officer would not let King George VI into an intelligence meeting. When asked to explain himself by a superior officer, he said he did not know the King was a BIGOT."

Eisenhower smiled his famous smile. "That sounds like typical British bullcrap."

"Yes sir, as you say."

"Well keep me informed captain of any new events. As for now I have a meeting to attend."

"Yes sir," said Abe as he saluted. He reached the door. Eisenhower said, "Oh captain, I am not convinced that our colonel is dead; keep searching."

"Yes sir."

Eisenhower lights a cigarette and pours a cup of coffee from the sidebar. He speaks into the intercom, "Sergeant Miller bring me the file on a Lieutenant Colonel Henry Walker."

"Yes sir, right away," a voice said on the intercom.

A few minutes later the door opened, and in walked Sergeant Miller with a folder in hand. He placed it on the desk, "Anything else sir?"

"Have my car brought around sergeant, that will be all."

"Yes sir."

Eisenhower opens the file and begins to read. Lieutenant Colonel Henry Walker, age 26. Born in Austin, Texas 1918. "Young to be a Lieutenant Colonel, made rank fast, I was in my thirty's before I made that rank," said Eisenhower as he continued to read. Grew up on his parents farm outside of Austin, raised cattle and grew a variety of crops. They had a hard time during the depression, but not as hard as some others. They managed to keep the farm and with the crops they sold, they scraped by. He and his brother helped out with the chores. Between work on the farm and school there was not much time for anything else. The older brother who served in the navy that was killed at Pearl Harbor. Henry graduated from the University of Texas at Austin with a degree in structural engineering. He married his high school sweetheart by the name of Alice and joined the Army in 1937, became commissioned through the OCS program. The marriage did not last; Alice could not become accustomed to military life. A major by 1942 and recently promoted to his present rank, he had decided to make the military his career. Decorated with a Bronze Star at Anzio while leading a team of engineers clearing the beach prior to the invasion. His father was a veteran of World War I, served with the

Big Red One in France as a Captain of an Infantry battalion.

Eisenhower laid the folder down. "Interesting fellow, good solider," he said.

A voice came on the intercom, "You car is here general."

"Thank you sergeant, I'll be right there."

David Dwight Eisenhower was born in Denison, Texas and was raised in Kansas. He graduated from West Point in 1915, in the class of the stars, so called because of the many classmates became generals later in their military service, including General Omar Bradley and General George Patton.

Second Lieutenant Eisenhower upon graduation requested an assignment in the Philippines, which was denied. He was instead posted in Texas.

When the US entered World War I, he immediately requested an overseas assignment but was denied and then assigned to Fort Leavenworth.

After the war, Eisenhower was promoted to major and assumed duties at Camp Meade, Maryland, commanding a battalion of tanks. His new expertise in tank warfare was strengthened by a close collaboration with George S. Patton and other senior tank leaders.

After completing that assignment he graduated from the Army War College in 1928 followed by a one-year assignment in France.

In 1932 Eisenhower was posted as chief military aid to General Douglas MacArthur. In 1935, he accompanied MacArthur to the Philippines, where he served as assistant military advisor to the Philippine government in developing their army.

Eisenhower was promoted to lieutenant colonel in 1936. He also learned to fly, making a solo flight over the Philippines in 1937 and obtained his private pilot's license in 1939.

Eisenhower returned the United States in December 1939 and was assigned as commanding officer of the 1st Battalion, 15th Infantry Regiment at Fort Lewis, Washington, later becoming the regimental executive officer.

In March 1941 he was promoted to colonel and assigned as chief of staff of the newly activated IX Corps, followed by promotion to brigadier general in October 1941.

After the Japanese attack on Pearl Harbor, Eisenhower was assigned to the General Staff in Washington, D.C., where he served until June 1942 with the responsibility for creating the major war plans to defeat Japan and Germany.

In November 1942, he was appointed Supreme Commander Allied Expeditionary Force of the North African Theater of Operations and was thereby promoted to major general. After that operation was completed, he was again promoted to lieutenant general.

In December 1943, President Roosevelt decided that Eisenhower would be the Supreme Allied Commander in Europe and that he would plan the invasion of France, which is his present role. Along with this reasonability came his fourth star.

2

The following day, Captain Abe reported to General Eisenhower.

"What have you got for me captain?"

"Not much new, general. We have swept the area several times, no other bodies found. The German E-boats run us out of there a few times."

"I'm sorry to hear that. Search one more day captain. Then if we don't find our missing colonel I'll declare him dead, body not recovered.

"Yes sir, we'll do our best."

"I would hate to think he is still alive out there, and we just have not found him, or worse yet the Germans captured him. With the deception plans in progress that would be very damaging. Operation Bodyguard has been in effect for several months now, I would hate to see all the effort we put into the plan destroyed."

"I don't think we need to worry about it, general."

"Easy for you to say captain, I'm the Supreme Commanding General, its my responsibility."

"I would hate to be in your shoes general."

Eisenhower smiles, lights a cigarette, "Well captain, that's part of the job. Sometimes I wonder if I am in the right job. But I do know if Operation Bodyguard fails, we are in deep trouble."

"Yes sir, I see what you mean."

"Report to me in the next 24 hours," Eisenhower said taking a seat behind his desk.

"Yes sir, will do."

The captain saluted and disappeared out the door.

Eisenhower poured himself a cup of coffee and lit a cigarette. He blows out a long stream of smoke and said to himself, "Yes, it is my responsibility."

The deception strategy code name Bodyguard, consisted of two parts; Operation Fortitude North and Fortitude South, with the aim of misleading the German high command as to the location of the imminent invasion.

Both Fortitude plans involved the creation of phantom field armies based in Edinburgh and the south of England, which threatened Norway with Fortitude North and Pas de Calais with Fortitude South. The operation was intended to divert Axis attention away from Normandy.

Operation Bodyguard's principle objective was to ensure the Germans would not increase troop presence in Normandy by promoting the appearance that the Allied forces would attack in other locations.

The planning of Operation Fortitude came under the auspices of the London Controlling Section (LCS), a secret body set up to manage Allied deception strategy during the war. However, the execution of each plan fell to the various theatre commanders, in this case this was the Supreme Headquarters Allied Expeditionary Force (SHAEF) under General Dwight D. Eisenhower. The LCS retained responsibility for what was called 'Special Means', the use of diplomatic channels and double agents.

The Fortitude South plan was produced in early January 1943 and aimed to counter the likelihood that the Germans would notice invasion preparations in the South of England. The intention was to create the impression that an invasion was aimed at the Pas de Calais. Once the real invasion had landed, six fictional divisions would keep this threat to Calais alive. The Fortitude South plan would be implemented, at an operational level, by the invasion force of the 21st Army Group under the command of General Bernard Montgomery.

Fortitude South invented an entire new field army. The First United States Army Group (FUSAG) commanded by General George Patton was a skeleton formation formed for administrative purposes, but never used. However, the Germans had discovered its existence through radio intercepts, which convinced them that the invasion would come in the Pas de Calais area.

Fortitude South main aim was to present a threatening appearance of an invasion at Pas de Calais by the fictional 1st U.S. Army Group. France was the crux of the Bodyguard plan, as the most logical choice for an invasion, the Allied high command had to mislead the German defenses in a very small geographical area. The Pas de Calais offered a number of advantages over the chosen invasion site, such as the shortest crossing of the English Channel and the quickest route into Germany. As a result, German command took steps to heavily fortify that area of coastline. The Allies decided to amplify this belief of a Calais landing.

General Montgomery, commanding the Allied landing forces, knew that the crucial aspect of any invasion was the ability to enlarge a beachhead into a full front. He also had only limited divisions at his command, 37 compared to around 60 German formations.

Another aim of Fortitude South was to give the impression of a much larger invasion force, the FUSAG forming in South-East England, to achieve tactical surprise in the Normandy landings and, once the invasion had occurred, to mislead the Germans into thinking it a diversionary tactic with Calais the real objective.

The Germans were allowed to construct a misleading order of battle for Allied forces. To mount a massive invasion of Europe from England, military planners had little choice but to stage units around the country with those that would land first nearest to the embarkation point. As a result of FUSAG's having been placed in the south-east, German intelligence would deduce that the center of the invasion force was opposite Calais, the point of the French closest to England and therefore a likely landing point.

To facilitate this deception, additional buildings were constructed; dummy aircraft and landing craft were placed around possible embarkation points. Patton paid many of these a visit along with a photographer. The Army encouraged the idea that these dummies were used to draw attention away from some of the other means of deception. Many of the dummies were rubber blow up kits of tanks, trucks, and other vehicles.

Fortitude North was designed to mislead the Germans into expecting an invasion of Norway. By threatening any weakened Norwegian defense, the Allies hoped to prevent or delay reinforcement of France following the Normandy invasion. The plan involved simulating a buildup of forces in northern England and political contact with Sweden.

A fictional Army, British Fourth Army, was created, headquartered in Edinburgh Castle. Unlike its Southern counterpart the deception relied primarily on 'Special Means' and fake radio traffic, since it was judged unlikely that German reconnaissance planes could reach Scotland unintercepted. False information about the arrival of troops in the area was reported by double agent Garbo. By broadcasting fake information, such as football scores, wedding announcements and nonexistent troops, Fortitude North was so successful that by late spring 1944, Hitler had thirteen army divisions in Norway.

For deceptions, the Allies had developed a number of methodologies, referred to as 'Special Means'. They included combinations of physical deceptions, fake wireless activity, leaks through diplomatic channels, and double agents. Fortitude used all of these techniques to various extents. For example, Fortitude North relied heavily on wireless transmissions while Fortitude South utilized the Allies network of double agents.

Physical deception was designed to mislead the enemy with nonexistent units through fake infrastructure and equipment, such as dummy landing craft, dummy airfields, and decoy lighting.

Controlled leaks of information through diplomatic channels, which might be passed on via neutral countries to the Germans was also helpful.

Wireless traffic was used to mislead the enemy where wireless traffic was created to simulate actual units.

Use of German agents controlled by the Allies through the Double Cross System were utilized to send false information to the German intelligence services.

One of these agents Juan Pujol Garcia was a Spanish citizen who deliberately became a double agent against Germany. He relocated to England to carry out fictional spying activities for the Nazis, and was known by the British codename Garbo and the German codename Alaric Arabel.

Garcia had the distinction of receiving military decorations from both sides during the war, gaining both the Iron Cross from Germany and a Member of the Order of the British Empire from Britain.

Garcia decided to become a spy for the Allies and contacted the British and American intelligence agencies, but each rejected his offer.

Undeterred, he created a false identity as a fanatically pro-Nazi Spanish government official and successfully became a German agent. He was instructed to travel to England and recruit additional agents; instead he moved to Lisbon and created bogus reports from a variety of public sources.

Although the information would not have withstood close examination, Garcia soon established himself as a trustworthy agent. He began inventing fictional sub-agents who could be blamed for false information and mistakes.

The Allies finally accepted Garcia when the Germans spent considerable resources attempting to hunt down a fictional convoy. He moved to England and spent the rest of the war expanding the fictional work, communicating at first by letter to the German handlers and later by radio. Eventually the Germans were funding a network of twenty-seven fictional agents.

Garcia had a key role in the success of Operation Fortitude, the deception operation intended to mislead the Germans about the timing and location of the invasion of Normandy. The false information Garcia supplied helped persuade the Germans that the main attack would be in the Pas de Calais, so that they kept a large force there to meet that attack.

Henry Walker woke in an early morning mist with the sea calm, moving the raft in a slow gentle way. He looked around through bleary eyes but with the mist and fog he could only see a few feet in front of the raft. He looked at his watch, it had stopped working so he took it off, attempted to wind the stem but as he pulled it out, it broke off. He put it up to his ear, there is no ticking. He throws the watch into the sea in disgust. "Damn cheap watch."

He sits and wonders how long he has been adrift, maybe as long as two days, but there is no real way to know for sure. He props himself on his knees and urinates over the side. He feels sick to his stomach but has no feeling to have a bowel movement, that might come later.

He feels for his wound on the side of his head, the dressing is still there but is now soaked mostly by seawater. He removes the dressing and feels the wound; it has stopped bleeding, so he decides to leave it open. There is about two inches of water in the bottom of the raft. He cupped a hand full of water and washed away the blood from the side of his face.

In one corner, he finds the emergency pack that contains food, canned water and signal flares. In one pouch, he finds a dry biscuit, and in another some bully beef, a field ration found in the British Army and not very popular. He takes a bite of the meat. "Not steak but what the hell, I'm hungry," he said to himself. He chews on the biscuit and makes a face and continues to eat. After eating the rations he opens one of the cans of water, drinks it down and throws the empty can in the sea. He makes a quick check on the other rations stored in the container. He estimates there is enough food and water there for at least another week, maybe even longer if he had to spread it out.

He moves back into the corner of the raft and examines his left foot and found his ankle swollen. He attempts to move his foot back and forth but pain stopped that.

He believes that the ankle is not broken; at least he hoped not, but was only a sprain, however it is painful.

He noticed in the first aid pack there is a small tube marked morphine tablets.

He finds them, takes one without water and sits back thinking of what happened with the exercise. What went wrong? How did the German E-boats find them so quick, and why didn't they have more protection from the British Navy?

His mind wanders to all those men in the water and on the landing crafts, "Did any survive, am I the only one?" He lays his head back and drifts off to asleep.

"Captain Abe is here to see you general," a voice said in the intercom.

"Send him in," replied Eisenhower.

Captain Abe marched in to find Eisenhower behind his desk, cigarette in hand with a pile of papers to work through. The captain saluted, "Good morning general."

"Good morning captain, take a seat. If you want some coffee, help yourself at the side bar."

"No thank you sir, already had several cups. You asked me to report to you about our disaster.

"Yes I did, and what have you to report?"

"I'm afraid not anything new general. We have searched for three days now and have recovered most of the dead. Some will never be recovered, inside the ships, which makes recovery impossible. Also we have recovered nine of the BIGOTs but the tenth is still missing."

"That bothers me captain. No knowing what happened to him is of great concern to me. What if he survived and the Germans have him? They'll squeeze information out of him to be sure. There is only so much torture a man can take before he breaks."

"I understand your concern general but I doubt he is still alive. He probably went down in one of the ships, we will never know."

"Your probably right captain but I am still uneasy about it. At any rate I'll cut orders to declare him dead, body not recoverable."

"How do we handle the families of the ones that died? We need to notify the families of how they died, a lot of letters to write."

"This has been a top secret exercise captain. As you know, the survivors have been sworn to secrecy, we want to keep it that way. Letters will be sent out to the families after the invasion takes place. The families will be notified that their fathers and sons were killed during the invasion, fighting for their country. That's how that will be handled. It is for the best interest of the Army to be handled in that manner."

"Yes sir, I see."

Eisenhower takes a sip of coffee, sits the cup down, "Any breach of the protocol by anyone will have serious consequences. I will court-marshal anyone who does not abide by my orders. Is that clear captain?"

"Yes sir, very clear."

"Good then, return to your duties, you are dismissed."

3

James Ferguson was busy reading his morning paper when John Masterman entered through the open door. "Margie said you were here and to go on in," said Masterman.

Margie is Ferguson's secretary, a yeoman in the British Auxiliary Women's Service. She has been with the Brigadier since her pilot husband was killed in the Battle of Britain, the air battle of 1940.

"Well, have seat my boy," said Ferguson as he limped over to the sidebar using his cane as an aid to his left leg, a product of the first war, which left him unfit for military service in this war but did allow him a position in the British intelligence service.

"What brings you out this early?" Ferguson said pouring two cups of tea.

"You asked to see me this morning Brigadier," Masterman said using the man's military title.

"Yes, of course I did," Ferguson, said handing over a cup of tea. "I wanted to pick your brain about the tragic event that happened the other day, most tragic indeed."

"You are speaking of the landing rehearsal that went wrong?"

"Yes indeed my boy, a disaster of great proportion. Lost over 700 men, mostly yanks, and a few of our lads I understand."

"That is also my understanding sir, a terrible thing."

Ferguson takes his seat. "What I don't understand is how the Germans found out about the exercise, someone may have tipped them off. How about that Garbo fellow? He was working for the German intelligence before you turned him into a double agent. Maybe he is working both sides, what you say?"

"I don't think so Brigadier, he's been on the up and up since he entered my double cross program. He would have much to lose if he turned on us."

"I see," said Ferguson lighting a large cigar. "Then you trust him?"

"Yes sir, I do, but one never knows. I'll check it out with one of my other agents."

"And who might that be?"

"I'll use George."

"George is it? And is he trustworthy?"

"Completely sir, I have used him before to keep tabs on Garbo."

"Oh yes, I remember something about that. Then if there was no leak about the exercise, then what happened?"

"Not real sure Brigadier. My guess is that the E-boats just happened to be at the right place and went to work."

"Went to work indeed. I wonder how Eisenhower is going to explain to the families how their people died in an exercise?"

"I imagine he will come up with something."

Ferguson blew out a long stream of smoke, "I'm sure you are right, but I would hate to have that job."

"Yes sir. Not easy to write all those letters."

"Indeed," Ferguson said puffing on his cigar. He waved the cigar in small circles.

"Nice cigar, got some from the PM, Cuban you know. I was with him last evening. He was concerned about what happened, wanted to know more about it. I'll see him later today and report your findings."

"I hope my information will satisfy him."

"I'm sure it will, since that's all we have."

Masterman nods his head as he lights his pipe. "Well I must be off to the office."

"Very well my boy. How about a late lunch at the club, say around 1400 hours?

"That will be fine Brigadier, see you then."

"Oh, before you go, do you have any information on this George fellow in your briefcase? I would like to know more about him."

"Yes, of course Brigadier," Masterman said as he opened his case. "I have a file here that should contain the information you need."

"Very good my boy, see you later at the club."

James Ferguson has a position of Chief of Operations in British Intelligence, also known as MI-5. He began work shortly after the Great War had left him unable to continue in the military. After his discharge he kept the title of Brigadier as a matter of cursory. Wounded by shellfire in the Argonne forest left him with a permanent limp and continuous pain that caused him to indulge in fair amounts of whiskey. Ferguson is a large man, somewhat untidy in appearance; the only hint of anything military is his Guards tie.

Ferguson preferred to work at home when possible in the splendor of his Cavendish Square flat, a much better surroundings than the drab MI-5 headquarters on Baker Street. It is rare that he visits anyone except when called to the Prime Minister. He prefers to have people come to him as a matter of convenience.

After the second war started it became apparent that the British Intelligence Service was in much-needed upgrade. John Masterman met the Brigadier at a social function in London shortly after the war started. Ferguson was immediately impressed by Masterman's knowledge of how the German Intelligence Service functioned. It seems Masterman had spent a number of years in Germany as a service officer to the British consulate. Masterman was fluent in German and had a working knowledge of French and Spanish.

Ferguson offered him a position in MI-5 and he was soon in charge of a group named 'Twenty Committee.' The number 20 in Roman numerals is XX, which became the double cross program, as it was known. This program's main function was to turn German agents who came to England into double agents working for the British.

This was a system based on an internal memo drafted by Masterman where he criticized the long-standing policy of arresting and sending to trial all enemy agents discovered by MI-5. Several had offered to defect to Britain when captured; such requests were invariably turned down. The memo Masterman wrote advocated turning captured agents wherever possible, and use them to mislead enemy intelligence agencies. This turned into a massive and well-tuned system of deception.

Beginning with the capture of an agent named Owens, code name Snow, MI-5 began to offer enemy agents the chance to avoid prosecution and thus the possibility of the death penalty, if they would work as British double agents.

Agents who agreed to this were supervised by MI-5 in transmitting bogus intelligence back to the German secret service, the Abwehr. This necessitated a large-scale organization effort, since the information had to appear valuable but actually be misleading. The high level committee was formed to provide this information; the day-to-day operation was delegated to a subcommittee, Twenty Committee.

Through 1940 and 1941, German Intelligence Service or Abwehr as it was known, would send messages regularly unknown to them alerting the Twenty Committee to impending arrivals of new agents in Britain. The messages were intercepted by the code breakers at Bletchley Park and turned over to MI-5.

Masterman viewed double agents who had pretended to work for the enemy of great value in counterespionage, thereby penetrating the enemy's secret service and learning about its methods of operation and discovering its intentions.

By July 1942 Masterman had turned almost the entire German agents operating in England into double agents. Reports from German's own high level intelligence, captured in decoded messages had persuaded the British that the seemingly impossible was in fact true. What began as a purely defensive effort to safeguard Britain from German espionage and detect Nazi plans turned into one of Britain's most effective secret weapons of the war. The most successful effort was the breaking of coded messages enciphered using the German's super secret Enigma machine.

The Enigma machine was invented by the German engineer Arthur Scherbius. The machine was a combination of mechanical and electrical subsystems. The mechanical subsystem consisted of a keyboard; a set of rotating disks and rotors arranged adjacently along a spindle; and one of various stepping components to turn at least one rotor with each key press.

The parts acted in such a way as to form a varying electrical circuit. When a key was pressed, one or more rotors moved to form a new rotor configuration, and a circuit was completed. Current flowed through various components in the new configuration, ultimately lighting one display lamp, which showed the new output letter.

A German Enigma operator would be given a plaintext message to encrypt. For each letter typed in, a lamp indicated a different letter according to a random substitution, based upon the wiring of the machine. The letter indicated by the lamp would be recorded as the enciphered substitution.

The action of pressing a key also moved the rotor so that the next key press used a different electrical pathway, and thus, a different substitution would occur. For each key pressed, there was rotation of at least the right-hand rotor, giving a different substitution alphabet. This continued for each letter in the message until the message was completed and a series of substitutions, each different from the others, had occurred to create a cryphertext from plaintext.

The cyphertext would then be transmitted as normal to an operator of another Enigma machine. The operator would key in the text, and for every key press, the reverse substitution would occur, and the plain text message would emerge.

British code breakers were regularly reading the orders and messages of the highest levels of the German command. The Enigma decrypts provided an incomparable window into German military plans and thinking.

What Masterman realized was that with some fiendishly clever thinking, the Enigma decrypts could be something much more than just a source of intelligence about enemy plans; they were the key to manipulating the enemy. To put it in other terms, in providing a window into the Germans' minds, the Enigma messages could also show the best way to mess with their minds. And as the man running the double agents, Masterman was just the right person to do that messing.

Masterman had spent most of World War I interned in Germany as an enemy alien, which led to his fluency in the language. Unquestionably an intellectual, he was an outstanding teacher and historian at Oxford when he was drafted into the British Army's Intelligence Corps in 1940.

At the start of the war, the conventional view of double agents was that they were spies who pretended to work for the enemy and their main value was in counterespionage, that is penetrating the enemy's secret service, learning about its methods of operation, and discovering its intentions. Several of the first double agents to come under British control had been playing both sides on their own initiative.

To run the double agents, Masterman's instructions to his committee members were to keep the agents sufficiently well fed with accurate information so as not to lose the confidence of the enemy; to control as many of the agents in England as they can, in order to make the enemy feel that the ground is covered and they need not send any more of whose arrival the committee might not be aware of and finally to carefully study the questionnaires submitted to them by their Abwehr handlers, to mislead the enemy on a big scale at the appropriate moment.

The double cross operation quickly discovered the characteristics of the radio signals the Abwehr was using to communicate with its agents from its base station in Hamburg, time of day, and message headings. This allowed British code breakers to identify other radio traffic between the Abwehr and its spies throughout Europe.

By April 1940 the code breakers at Britain's secret establishment at Bletchley Park were beginning to read Abwehr traffic. Throughout 1941, Abwehr messages were regularly alerting the Twenty Committee to the impending arrival of new agents in Britain. Most were dropped by parachute; others came ashore on rubber rafts launched from U-boats.

Not every captured agent was a suitable candidate to become a double agent, Masterman noted. It would have looked strange to the Germans if all their agents had arrived safely, evading capture, and gone to work efficiently filing espionage reports. And it was vital that a spy be apprehended almost immediately after arrival to be sure he hadn't already communicated with Germany and possibly warned of impending capture.

Another problem that limited the usefulness of the double agents was the constant fear that any cooked up reports sent back by the controlled agents would be contradicted by other German agents who had slipped in undetected, possibly endangering the whole scheme.

Then came the agent code named 'Garbo' who was to become one of Masterman's most effective agents. In February 1942, British intelligence officers found themselves puzzling over a series of agent reports of superb inaccuracy that began appearing in Enigma messages being sent to Berlin from the Abwehr station in Madrid. They purported to be from an agent in Britain, and dealt mainly with merchant shipping convoys from the British Isles to the Mediterranean. The only trouble was that none of the reported convoys corresponded with actual shipping movements.

The startling fact, though, was that these reports not only seemed to be taken with 100 percent seriousness by the spy's Abwehr masters; they also aligned precisely with a seemingly fantastic story that had been told to a British intelligence officer in Spain a few months earlier by a Spaniard named Juan Garcia, who approached him offering to become a British spy.

Garcia had first tried to become a British agent right after the war broke out and was rebuffed. After he had been turned down he hit on the idea that maybe the British would find him more valuable if he first established himself with the Abwehr as a German agent, and then offered to double cross them. That is exactly what he was doing.

After using some faked documents to persuade the Abwehr station in Madrid that he could infiltrate his way into Britain, he had traveled to Lisbon, Portugal. There, armed with nothing more than a tour guide of Britain, a Portuguese publication on the British fleet, and whatever technical journals he could find in the public library, he invented a series of subagents and a raft of imaginative reports that he duly mailed to his Abwehr handlers in Madrid.

To explain the Lisbon postmarks, he told his Abwehr control that he had recruited as a courier an airline employee who had agreed to take his dispatches from England and drop them in the post in Portugal during his regular flights there. It all sounded ludicrous to the British, but the Enigma decrypts changed everything. They confirmed every key point of Garcia's story. Moreover, they showed, incredibly, that the Germans had complete, unquestioning confidence in him.

Now fully convinced of his value as a double agent, the British smuggled Garcia into England and was given the code name 'Garbo.'

Ferguson poured himself a large whisky and lit one of Churchill's cigars. He opened the file and began to read.

Fritz Kolbe was born in Berlin to middle-class parents. Kolbe was conscripted into the German army as a civilian worker in October 1917. He was assigned to a telegraph unit and then an engineer battalion. He was employed by the German foreign ministry in 1925 as a clerk. In 1936 he was posted as a mid-level diplomat in Madrid. After Madrid, Kolbe was stationed in Warsaw before returning to Berlin in 1937.

By diligence and skill, Kolbe earned the trust of the people he reported. He was given positions of increasing responsibility in the Foreign Office, however he refused to join the Nazi party.

In 1941, Kolbe was assigned to Karl Ritter who served in the Foreign Office as a liaison with the military. Ritter was located near Hitler's headquarters. Reports from foreign diplomats and up to over a 100 reports a week from German consulates and embassies were directed to Berlin for Ritter. Kolb's duty was to read them all and reply important ones on to Ritter. He also reviewed and summarized news articles from foreign press. Kolbe realized that his activities were likely under surveillance, given the importance of the work and the fact that Kolbe still would not join the Nazi party.

In late 1941, Kolbe became determined to actively help defeat the Nazis. Kolbe passed information from cables to the French Resistance, particularly when it could save someone's life or prevent an arrest. In some cases, the information was sent to London.

In 1943, an opportunity for espionage arose when a fellow anti-Nazi in the ministry reassigned Kolbe to higher-grad work as a diplomatic courier. Later in 1943 he traveled to Bern Switzerland with the diplomatic bag. While there, he offered mimeographed secret documents to the British embassy. British MI-5 realized they had an agent of the highest quality. Kolbe moved to England after an offer was made from the British Intelligence service to become an agent in their service. Kolbe then became an agent under the control of John Masterman and given the code name of George.

Ferguson laid the file aside and poured another whisky. "Interesting fellow this George. I can see now why John has made use of him. Jolly good show."

Walker woke to the sounds of sea gulls. He rubbed his eyes and strained to look through the fog, it was early morning. He ate two biscuits and drank a can of water. The sea was calm although the raft moved fairly fast along. He threw the empty can in the water, turned to see a hole in the fog. There seemed to be a landmass ahead. He blinked and rubbed his eyes to look again. "Looks like land to me, that must be France," he said leaning back. He checked the hidden pocket inside of his shirt for the blue capsule that had been given to all BIGOT personnel. If captured, it was expected for you to take the pill to avoid interrogation and give up vital information about the invasion.

His head wound was still giving him a good amount of pain and his ankle was not much better. He decided to take another morphine pill.

After about twenty minutes his pain eased, which allowed him to settle back and drift off to sleep as the raft carried him along.

Helen Wilkerson has lived on Alderney, one of the Channel Islands all her life. Her grandfather settled there, built a manor with a league of land and raised cattle. Her father owned a lifeboat rescue service and also ran the family business.

He and a crew went out one day to rescue a fishing vessel in distress in very high seas. He and two other crewmembers never came back, drowned when the boat was swamped by a large wave.

Helen is a young twenty-five year old blond that resembles her mother in every way. He mother passed away several years ago from an illness that was never known. The doctor said it might have been cancer.

She continues to take care of a few head of cattle; the Germans have taken most of them since their occupation. She lives alone in the manor and does most of the chores, feeding the chickens and tending the garden. There is a handyman that comes by when needed to work the heavier things, his name is Fred Wilson.

Fred lives down the road in a small house of his parents. Fred was born and raised on the island and knows it well. There is a small amount of land behind the house where Fred tends to a few head of cattle. He also cares for chickens and pigs. He has a rather large garden that keeps him busy. He appears to be self-sufficient, therefore living off the land.

As her usual habit in the mornings after a light breakfast, Helen and her Labrador retriever, Roger, take a walk down at the beach since the area is only a short distance from the manor.

On his morning she walked along while Roger ran in and out of the surf. She noticed something strange in the distance, an object on the beach, it seems to be stuck there. As she gets closer she can see it is a raft, there is an arm visible.

She decides to take a closer look and when she did, there is someone lying there in the bottom of the raft.

She moves closer and puts her hand on the man's shoulder. "Are you all right?" She said shaking his shoulder. There is no response, now she is thinking, this man might be dead. She checks for a pulse at the neck, there is one, a good strong one.

Again she calls out, "Are you all right?" Shaking his shoulder.

Suddenly the man stirs, opens his eyes and looks at her in a surprised look. "Who are you?" He asked in a slurred voice. "Where am I?" What's going on?"

"Are you all right?" Helen asked again.

"A little banged up." Walker said sitting up. "Who are you and where am I, is this France?"

"I am Helen Wilkerson, and no, this is not France, this is Alderney Island in the channel."

"One of the channel islands?"

"Yes that right."

"Are there any Germans here?"

"Yes, we have been occupied since the beginning of the war, mainly by the Kriegsmarine. An E-boat station is not far from here."

"Well that's just great."

"Who are you?" She asked.

"I'm Lieutenant Colonel Henry Walker, United States Army."

"Oh, I see, and you are hurt."

"Head wound and a painful ankle."

"You will need treatment for that."

"Are you going to turn me in to the Germans?"

"No, I think not, but let me help you. We can go to my place, I have first aid material and food."

"That's real kind of you," he said as he tried to stand. He collapsed as his ankle gave out. "Looks like I can't walk."

"I will go and get the horse and cart, it's only a short distance. I'll be right back, don't go anywhere." She then laughed slightly she realized what she had said.

"I'll be right here," he said as he pulled his .45 from his shoulder holster.

Helen returned to the manor and got one of the horses out of the corral. She located the harness in the barn and put it on the horse. Next she attached the horse to a two-wheel cart just as Fred the handy man came around from the barn.

"What's going on missy?" He always called her missy, a trait some older men name a young woman.

"Oh Fred, I'm glad you're here. There is a man, an American Army man on the beach in a raft. He's been hurt, I need to bring him to the house, and you can help me."

"Yes missy, get in the cart and we'll go."

In a short time they reach the raft to fine Walker still in the raft holding his .45.

"This is Fred, a friend of mine," She said.

Walker nods his head as Fred comes near.

"Nice to meet you sir, I'm here to help you, don't' worry."

"Yeah, I can use some help, thanks," Walker, replied.

They helped Walker into the cart, Helen climbed in the back with him, and then Fred led the horse away from the beach.

"You say the Germans have a base here. Do they have patrols out?"

"No, not really" She answered. "Sometimes some hike around the island for recreation I suppose. At times they use my manor as a meeting place for the officers in charge. And also they have parties, so they use my main living area, mainly when they have a high official guest."

"That's just great, and I'm there as your guest."

"Not to worry, I have a secret place to which you can stay in."

"Really? How is that?"

"My father built it before he had a rescue accident. It was originally a child's room to be next to the bedroom, the wall was not there, it was all open. He rebuilt it for me in case I ever needed to be safe from the Nazis. He put in the wall and secret panel. I have never used it since they leave me be. I let them use my manor for their functions."

"Oh, I see."

"That however, does not mean I like them."

"I'm glad to hear that."

They arrive at the manor. "Lets go around to the back Fred," Helen said. "Inside the downstairs closet, there are a pair of crutches, bring them Fred."

Fred does as he is told, in a few minutes he returns with a pair of crutches. They help Walker out of the cart and on to the crutches.

"This way," Helen said, as she helps Walker along.

Once inside the house, they help Walker up to the second floor. In the master bedroom, Helen pressed a place on the wall near the bed, a panel opened and she nodded for Walker to follow, which he did.

She turned on a light and motioned for Walker to the bed in the corner of the room. The room was about a standard size room and no windows, with a bed in the corner, a small closet, a table with two chairs and shelves on one wall. There was a bathroom with a shower.

"I think you will be comfortable here," Helen said.

"Not bad for a hideout," replied Walker.

"Lay down on the bed and rest, I'll find some clothes for you to change in and also I want to dress your wound."

Walker lays back on the bed, "This is nice, real nice."

Helen returned in a few minutes with a shirt, pants and underwear. "These belonged to my father but they should fit. Fred will assist you with the shower. I've asked him to place a chair in there so it will easier for you. I'll come back after you shower and dress your wound and bring you something to eat." She smiles and leaves.

As Helen stated, Fred helped Walker with his shower and back to his bed. A half hour later Helen returned with a ham and cheese sandwich and an arm full of dressing material. She examined his head wound and examined his ankle.

"I believe that's just a sprained ankle, need to stay off of it for awhile." She then carefully dressed his head wound. "There, that should do it." She said smiling.

"Thank you, you have been very kind," he said reaching for the sandwich.

"You did a good job. You must have some medical training."

"I started nursing school briefly in England before the war but I came home when my father had his accident."

"Oh I see. I'm sorry about your father."

"I miss him very much."

"I am sure you do."

"Just how did you get into this shape, where did you come from?"

"From the sea," He answered with a smile.

"Oh don't be silly, I know that, but what happened to you?"

"I can't tell you that, sorry."

"Oh I see, a secret thing."

"Yes, something like that."

"Well, finish your sandwich and get some rest. There are some magazines on the nightstand and a pitcher of water. There is a buzzer button there if you need me. We'll talk later; I have chores to do now. This evening I will bring you some stew, I make a good stew."

Walker nods head his with a mouth full of food. As Helen reaches the door, he said, "Good sandwich."

After she leaves, Walker placed the .45 in the nightstand's drawer. He wanted it close at hand. In his mind he was not sure if he could trust her. She could easily turn him over to the Germans for a reward and if that was to be, then he had his .45 and the capsule. He looked at a magazine for a short time, then sank back into the pillow and was fast asleep.

It was five in the morning when Heinrich Himmler got out of his car and entered Gestapo Headquarters at Prinz Albrechtstrasse in Berlin. He has a bad habit of turning up at unreasonable hours, which meant that, in a way, his appearance was not unexpected. Guards sprang to attention as entered. He wore full black dress uniform as Reichsfuhrer-SS and his face was as blank as usual.

He went upstairs, turned along the corridor and entered his office suite. In the anteroom, secretary Elsa, in field gray uniform of an SS Auxiliary, stood up behind her desk. A young women in her mid 20's with dark black hair pulled back into a bun. She had lost her husband in The Battle of Britain and now felt her duty to serve the Reich.

"Good morning Herr Reichsfuhrer," She said standing ramrod straight.

"Yes, yes," answered Himmler in his usual abrupt manner.

"Is Strumbannfuhrer Rossemann in the building?" Himmler asked.

"I saw him having breakfast in the canteen, Reichsfuhrer."

"Send for him at once."

"Yes, right away Reichsfuhrer."

Himmler went into his office, placed his briefcase on his desk and went to the window, where he stood looking out. After awhile, there was a knock at the door. The young man who entered was in black uniform and the silver cuff title on his sleeve carried the legend, RFSS, Reichsfuhrer der SS, the cuff title of Himmler's personal staff. He clicked his heels.

"At your orders, Reichsfuhrer."

" Ah yes, Rossemann." Himmler stood behind his desk. "You had the duty last night? You are due to go home?"

"Yes Reichsfuhrer."

"I'd appreciate it if you could stay a few minutes longer."

"Of course, Reichsfuhrer. My pleasure to be of service."

"Very good Rossemann. You are a good soldier."

"Thank you Reichsfuhrer."

Himmler moved to the window and looked out and was silent for a few minutes. He then turned, walked to his desk and sat down. "I have been trying to locate Oberfuhrer Schellenberg, without success, I might add. He is probably on one of his secret missions that he has a fancy to favor. At any rate I want you to find him for me and have him meet me at Wewelsburg as soon as possible. I will be there for the next several days. I have an important thing to discuss with him, very important. Make it a point to him. That is all, you are dismissed."

"As you order Reichsfuhrer.

Rosseman gave a stiff-arm salute and marched out the door. Himmler nodded and returned to his papers.

Himmler was born in Munich and attended school in Landshut, a small town in Bavaria, where his father was deputy principal. In 1915, he began training with the Landshut Cadet Corps. His father used his connections with the royal family to get Himmler accepted as an officer candidate, and he enlisted with the reserve battalion of the 11th Bavarian Regiment in December 1917.

In November 1918, while Himmler was still in training, the war ended with Germany's defeat, denying him the opportunity to become an officer or to see combat.

After the war, Himmler studied agronomy at the Munich Technische Hochschule following a brief apprenticeship on a farm. He joined the Nazi Party the following year. As a member of the SA unit, Himmler was involved in the Beer Hall Putsch, an unsuccessful attempt by Hitler and the Nazi Party to seize power in Munich.

Himmler took advantage of the disarray in the party following Hitler's arrest in the wake of the Beer Hall Putsch. From mid-1924 he worked under Gregor Strasser as party secretary and propaganda assistant.

Traveling all over Bavaria agitating for the party, he gave speeches and distributed literature. Placed in charge of the party office in Lower Bavaria by Strasser from late 1924, he was responsible for integrating the area's membership with the Nazi Party. That same year, he joined the Schtzstaffel as an SS-Fuhrer Leader.

Upon the resignation of SS commander Erhard Heiden in 1929, Himmler assumed the position of Reichsfuhrer-SS with Hitler's approval. By 1930 Himmler had persuaded Hitler to run the SS as a separate organization.

Over the next few years, he developed the SS from a mere 2900-man battalion into a powerful group with its own military, and following Hitler's orders, set up and controlled the Nazi concentration camps. He is known to have good organizational skills and for selecting highly subordinates, such as Reinhard Heydrich in 1931.

From 1943 forward, he is both Chief of German Police and Minister of the Interior, overseeing all internal and external police and security forces, including the Gestapo.

4

In Westphalia, in the small town of Wewelsburg, is the castle of that same name which Himmler had taken over from the local government soon after he had become Reichsfuhrer. His original intentions had been to convert it into a school for Reich SS leaders, but by the time builders had finished; he had created a Gothic monstrosity. The castle had three wings, tower, a moat, and in the southern wing Himmler had his own apartment. In one wing, there is an enormous dinning hall where selected members of the SS would meet in a kind of court of honor. The whole thing had been influenced by Himmler's obsession with King Arthur and the Knights of the Round Table.

Ten miles away on an April morning, SS-Oberfuhrer Walter Schellenberg is smoking a cigarette in the back of the Mercedes, which is speeding him toward the castle. He'd received the order from Rossemann the night before to meet Himmler as soon as possible. The reason was not specified. An order from Himmler is one that should not be dismissed.

Schellenberg had been at Wewelsburg on several occasions, had even inspected the castle's plans at SD headquarters, so he knew it well. He also knew that the only men to sit around the table with the Reichsfuhrer were clowns like Himmler himself who believed all the nonsense about Saxon superiority. The fact that King Arthur had been Romano-British engaged in a struggle against Saxon invaders made the whole thing even more nonsense, but Schellenberg had long since ceased to be amused by the excesses of the Third Reich.

Walter Schellenberg was born in Saarbrucken Germany. He moved with his family to Luxembourg when the French occupation of the Saar Basin after the First World War triggered an economic crisis in the Weimar Republic. Like many young men, Schellenberg was deeply affected by the economic woes, which befell Germany in the wake of the First World War.

Schellenberg returned to Germany to attend the University of Marburg and later the University of Bonn. He initially studied medicine, but soon switched to law. While in law school, Schellenberg performed some spy work for the SD. After graduating he joined the SS in 1933.

In 1935, Schellenberg met Obergruppenfuhrer Reinhard Heydrich and worked for him in the counter-intelligence department of the Sicherheitsdienst (SD). Beside his native German, Schellenberg also spoke French and English fluently.

As the Nazis tightened their grip on German society, Hitler and Reichsfuhrer-SS Heinrich Himmler determined that the SS and police departments should merge, a move, which Schellenberg fully supported.

Despite begin Heydrich's direct subordinate, Schellenberg skillfully ingratiated himself to Himmler by first delivering his intelligence reports to him instead of Heydrich.

In 1931, Himmler recruited Reinhard Heydrich as head of counter-intelligence. As the SS grew in importance, so did Heydrich's role in the Nazi Party. He was Himmler's right hand man, helping him and the Party maneuver for power.

In 1934, Heydrich was made head of the Gestapo, known as the SD, the feared secret police division of the SS.

Restoring order to the Reich Protectorate of Bohemia and Moravia was an important stepping-stone for Heydrich. Controlled by Germany since 1939, a year after the Munich Agreement had ceded

Czechoslovakia's western borders to Germany, the protectorate was a key source of coal and one of Europe's top arms manufacturing centers.

As the situation in the Czech protectorate deteriorated by fall 1941, Himmler and Hitler decided to send Heydrich in to clean things up.

Heydrich's experience running the Nazi secret police served him well when it came to cracking down on the already weak Czech opposition.

In the morning of May 26, 1942, Heydrich was assassinated by two Czech commandos while traveling in his open-topped Mercedes staff car on his way to work.

Shortly thereafter Schellenberg became head of the counter-intelligence service with the rank of Oberfuhrer-SS.

In 1940 Schellenberg was charged with compiling a blueprint for the occupation of Britain. The same year he was also sent to Portugal to intercept the Duke and Duchess of Windsor and try to persuade them to work for Germany. Schellenberg was supposed to offer them 50 million Swiss Francs to go to neutral Switzerland. The mission was a failure; he never got near the Duke and Duchess.

By the time he led the hunt for the Soviet spy ring, Red Orchestra, Schellenberg had become well known in the SS. He had arranged many plots of subterfuge and intelligence gathering.

Direct access to Himmler also made Schellenberg privy to some of the Reich's most sensitive material. For example, Schellenberg knew early on about the arrangement between Germany and Russia concerning the partition of Poland, an agreement that presaged the military invasion.

Once the Nazis invaded and occupied Polish territory, Schellenberg was entrusted with securing the rear areas for Himmler and Heydrich, which meant he oversaw the development of special commandos from the SD and Gestapo.

Another one of his areas of responsibility was counter-espionage, both within Germany and occupied territories, a task for which Schellenberg seemed well suited, given his penchant for intrigue.

Schellenberg's most successful mission was his part in the abduction of two British agents at the border town of Venlo, Netherlands. This became known as the Venlo Incident.

Captain Sigismund Best and Captain Richard Stevens had worked together in the first war, running agents in and out of Germany from the neutral Netherlands.

Best, a tall monocle-wearing figure who spoke flawless Dutch and German, had remained in Holland after the First World War. He had married a Dutch woman and cultivated contacts among the Dutch upper class while setting up an import-export business specializing in pharmaceuticals.

Shortly after the war started, the British Intelligence Service put in a parallel spy network known as the Z Organization. It was chiefly composed of British businessmen working in Europe. Best was asked to be the organization's Z man in Holland.

Best jumped at the chance to return to espionage work, and took up his old task of running agents into Germany. He convinced his old friend Stevens to join him so they could work together as a team.

On the orders of the Prime Minister, Winston Churchill, Best embarked on a dangerous game over a two-week period, when he begin talks with a group of Germans who claimed to be army officers plotting to bring Hitler down and end the war. In reality, Best's negotiating partners were top SD operatives playing a game orchestrated by Heydrich and authorized by the Fuhrer himself.

Best and Stevens began meetings with several German officers at a hotel in Venlo and agreed to have more meetings to discuss details. Realizing that the British had swallowed his bait, Heydrich raised the ante, assigning his brightest operative to direct the scheme, Walter Schellenberg.

Schellenberg sent two agents posing as German officers to meet Best and Stevens, where the German agents attracted the attention of the Dutch police. The meeting was cut short and the German agents returned to Germany.

For the next scheduled meeting, Schellenberg himself put in an appearance under the guise of a Major Schammel. As Schammel, Schellenberg demanded a full statement of Britain's real war aims as opposed to its publicly stated objectives. Best had carried such statements from the Prime Minister to the meeting in anticipation of such a request.

The statement explained that Hitler must be removed first before further progress could be made. In Berlin, however, Heydrich had decided to bring the Dutch game to an end. He directed Schellenberg to set one more meeting and bring it to a close.

Best and Stevens traveled to Venlo for the meeting with the man they knew as Schammel. However unknown to them, an SD snatch squad was lurking just a few yards over the border.

It is unclear just how much information Best and Stevens gave away to the SD during the first days of intensive interrogation. The more inexperienced Stevens cracked and told all that he knew. Incredibly, when captured, Stevens had been carelessly carrying a list of all the agents in Europe unencoded in his pocket.

The Venlo Incident had many consequences, nearly all negative from the British perspective. It crippled the spy network in Western Europe, since the service assumed that all its operatives had been betrayed, and withdrew them from the field. It now became Masterman's job to form a new and different spy network, the double cross system.

Schellenberg wore his black uniform of the SS instead of his usual civilian suit since it was more appropriate for the appearance with the Reichsfuhrer.

"What has Germany become?" He said to himself as the car took the road up to the castle. "I really do wonder who is running the lunatic asylum."

Schellenberg's main responsibility had always been intelligence work abroad. A series of brilliant intelligence coups had pushed him up the ladder rapidly. He did not consider himself a Nazi and looked down on some in the party as a bunch of sorry characters. He had many enemies but managed to survive for one reason, Himmler needed his brains and his talents, and that was enough.

Himmler received him in his private sitting room. Schellenberg was escorted there by an SS Sergeant in dress uniform and found Himmler's personal aide, Strumbannfuhrer Rossemann sitting at a table outside the door.

"Good afternoon Strumbannfuhrer," Schellenberg said.

Rossemann dismissed the sergeant. "A pleasure to see you Oberfuhrer," using his SS rank and coming to attention. "He is waiting, but I am afraid his mood is not good."

"I'll remember that," said Schellenberg.

Rossemann opened the door and Schellenberg entered a large room with a vaulted ceiling and lots of oak furniture. The Reichsfuhrer sat at an oak table working his way through a mound of papers.

"Oberfuhrer Schellenberg." He looked up. "You got here."

"I left Berlin the moment I received your message Reichsfuhrer. In what way may I serve you?"

"It has come to my attention that our Kreigsmarine had some action in the channel a few days ago, a source told me so. It seems some E-boats knocked out a combined Allied force in the middle of a landing exercise on the coast of northern England. An obvious exercise for the invasion that is to come. What do you know about it?"

"I believe you are correct Reichsfuhrer. The E-boats caught the landing crafts as they made their run to the shore. I understand there was a great loss of life."

"That is my understanding also," said Himmler. " I would very much like to know how the Kreigsmarine found out about this activity. Did we receive any information from one of our agents?"

"Not that I know of Reichsfuhrer. I believe the E-boats were out on a routine patrol when they happened upon the Allied exercise. They were in the right place at the right time."

" I suppose that may be," replied Himmler. "Have you had dealings with an agent named Garbo?" Asked Himmler standing from behind his desk.

"I know of him Reichsfuhrer, an Abwehr contact. A commercial attaché at the Portuguese Embassy in Lisbon. As far as I know, we have only used him occasionally. Garbo has use of a diplomatic bag to

London with messages for British Intelligence. We feel he is playing both sides of the fence as they say."

"We should keep an eye on this clown," Himmler said moving to the window to look out.

"As you say Reichsfuhrer."

Himmler turns and moves back to his desk. "The Allied exercise is most interesting. There could be some useful information there. Where any survivors captured?"

"No Reichsfuhrer, the British Navy recovered all of the dead and wounded that were in the water. Our E-boats interrupted their efforts several times but it appears they recovered everyone in the water, that is. Many men went down in the landing ships."

"Most unfortunate for them, I must say," said Himmler rubbing his nose.

"Now the question is, will they continue with the invasion plans since this disaster?" Stated Schellenberg.

"I am sure they will, Schellenberg. The question is where will they land? The Fuhrer and von Rundstead believe it will occur in the Pas de Calais area since it is the nearest point across. But then Rommel believes it will occur in the Normandy. But I believe Rommel is wrong, it is obvious to any fool it will be the Pas de Calais."

"Yes Reichsfuhrer, that is a question. It would be to our advantage if we knew."

"Of course, any fool can see that," Himmler said leaning back in his chair. "See what you can find out Schellenberg, and report to me any findings."

"As you order Reichsfuhrer."

"Now I must return to my paper work, you are dismissed."

5

"This is good stew," said Walker to Helen as she sat next to the bed watching him eat. "I think this is the best stew I've ever had."

"I'm glad you like it. I have more if you like, what about some more bread?"

"No this is fine, thank you. The bread is excellent."

"I bake it myself."

"You are a good cook Helen."

She collects the dishes and set them aside. "Let's check the dressing, I think a dressing change is in order."

She removes the old dressing and skillfully applies a new one. "That should do it, anything else I can do for you?"

"No, I'm fine. Unless you can find a way to get me out of here so I can return to England."

"That will be difficult colonel, with the Nazis right here."

"Please call me Henry, or use my middle name John. My mother always called me John."

"John it is then. Tell me, are you married?"

"No, not now. I was married once for a short time. She could not get accustomed to military life so we went our separate ways."

"I see, the military is your life and you are so young to be a colonel."

"Well, I'm just a half colonel," he replied with a smile.

"Did you have any kids?"

"No, no kids."

"Where are you from, John, I mean in the United States?"

"I'm from Texas, we have a farm outside of Austin, been in the family since my grandparents. My parents still run the place but hire outside help now that my brother and me are no longer there to help out."

"And what does your brother do now?"

"He was my older brother, Bob. He joined the Navy, killed at Pearl Harbor."

"Oh, I'm sorry. That must have been difficult. I know how it was when I lost my father and mother."

Walker nodded his head and was silent. He reached for the glass of water on the nightstand. Helen reached for it at the same time almost causing contact with his face by a mere inch. At that point Walker realized just how beautiful she really is.

She smiled, "Let me get that for you."

He drank a few swallows then gave the glass back to her. "Are you married?" He asked.

She smiled, "No, never had the time to find anyone. With the occupation and most of the population gone, there is not much chance of finding someone. All the young men are gone off to war."

"Must be lonely here by yourself.

"Oh, it's not so bad, I keep busy with the place, animals to take care of and such. And now I have you to take care of," she added with a big smile.

"You have been very kind to me."

"Well, I'm glad to help, after all, we are on the same side. You rest now; I'll be back later. Remember the buzzer if you need me. I have put the night pot next to the bed for your use."

"Thank you Helen."

"Good night John." And with that she left.

The planning for Operation Overlord, the invasion of France began in 1943.

Between May and June 1940, over 338,00 troops of the British Expeditionary Force and the French Army, trapped along the northern coast of France were rescued in the Dunkirk evacuation. After the German Army invaded the Soviet Union in June 1941, the

Soviet leader Joseph Stalin began pressing his allies for the creation of a second front in Western Europe.

In late 1942 the Soviet Union and the United States made a joint agreement to create a second front as early as 1943. However, British Prime Minister Winston Churchill persuaded President Franklin Roosevelt to postpone the promised invasion as, even with American help, the Allies did not have adequate forces for such activity.

Instead of an immediate invasion of France, the Western Allies staged an offensive in the Mediterranean Theatre of Operations, where British troops were already stationed. By mid-1943 the campaign in North Africa had been won. The Allies then launched the invasion of Sicily, and subsequently invaded Italy in September the same year. By then, Soviet forces were on the offensive and had won a major victory at the Battle of Stalingrad. The decision was then made to undertake a cross-channel invasion.

With four sites to consider, two were picked out as possible landing sites; Pas de Calais and Normandy. With the Pas de Calais being the closest point in continental Europe to Britain, the Germans considered it to be the most likely initial landing zone, so it was heavily fortified.

However, Pas de Calais offered few opportunities for expansion, as the area is bound by numerous rivers and canals, whereas landings on a broad front in Normandy would permit simultaneous threats against the port of Cherbourg, coastal ports further west in Brittany, and an overland attack towards Paris and eventually into Germany. Normandy was hence chosen as the landing site.

The amphibious landings are to be preceded by extensive aerial and naval bombardment and an airborne assault, landing 24,000 American, British, and Canadian airborne troops shortly after midnight the night before the land invasion. Allied infantry and armored divisions are scheduled to land at 06:30 hours on a stretch of the Normandy coast which will be divided into five sectors: Utah, Omaha, Gold, Juno and Sword. Where American forces would land on Utah and Omaha beaches, the British forces on Gold and Sword and the Canadians on Juno.

The Allies planned to launch the invasion 1 May 1944. The initial draft of the plan was accepted at the Quebec Conference in August 1943. General Eisenhower was appointed Commander of Supreme Headquarters Allied Expeditionary Force. General Bernard Montgomery was named as commander of the

21st Army Group, which comprised all of the land forces involved in the invasion.

On 31 December 1943 Eisenhower and Montgomery first saw the plan, which proposed amphibious landings by three divisions with two more divisions in support. The two generals immediately insisted that the scale of the initial invasion be expanded to five divisions, with airborne descents by three additional divisions, to allow a wider front and speed up the capture of Cherbourg. The need to acquire or produce extra landing craft for the expanded operation meant that the invasion had to be delayed to June.

General Eisenhower entered the conference room at his headquarters outside of London; the location was secret to all except to certain high-ranking officers. He walked to the head of the desk to find his main staff already there, seated at the table. Seated at the table were General Bernard Montgomery, Lieutenant General Omar Bradley, Admiral Bertram Ramsey, Air Chief Marshal Arthur Tedder, and Lieutenant General Walter Bedell Smith. They all stood as he entered.

"As you were gentlemen, please take your seats," Eisenhower said.

"I called this meeting to update you on certain information for the invasion planned as you know for June." He moves in front of a large map tacked to the wall. He picks up a long pointer stick and steps to the side of the map.

"As you can see the Normandy landing site is divided into five sectors: Utah, Omaha, Gold, Juno, and Sword. Prior to the infantry landing, the boys of the 2nd Ranger Battalion will take Pointe du Hoc, and that is no easy task I must add. They will have to climb a 100-foot cliff under fire to take out the big guns there. It is necessary to take out that artillery, because they can reach the beach where our boys will come in."

He taps the Utah sector on the map with his pointer. "The VII Corps will land here. This will consist of the 4th Infantry Division, and the 90th Infantry Division The 82nd Airborne and the 101st Airborne will make their drops earlier in the morning near Caen on the eastern flank to secure the Orne River bridges and north of Carentan on the western flank. This is to capture Carentan and St.Lo the first day, then cut off the Cotentin Peninsula and eventually capture the port facilities at Cherbourg. Omaha is assigned to the 1st Infantry Division and 29th Division, after they secure the beach; their mission is to work their way inland. The British at Sword and Gold Beaches and

Canadians at Juno Beach will protect the American flank and attempt to establish airfields near Caen. The British XXX Corps, consisting of the 50th Infantry Division will make a landing on Gold Beach. The British I Corps consisting of the 3rd Infantry Division will land on Sword Beach and the 3rd Canadian Infantry Division will land on Juno. The British 6th Airborne Division will jump to secure the flank of the 82nd. A secure lodgement will be established and made to hold all territory north of the Avranches-Falaise line within the first three weeks. Any comments, questions?"

Montgomery is the first to speak. "Well old boy, it seems to me the whole thing is quite complicated."

"Well Monty, do you have a solution to it?" "No, my dear fellow. It just looks a bit complicated with all the action you see. All these things need to happen on schedule which has a concern to me."

"You worry too much Monty," Eisenhower said lighting a cigarette. "Things will work out if the Germans took the bait that we will land at Pas de Calais, that is my concern. From our intelligence sources the Germans believe that the invasion will occur at Pas de Calais. They have moved massive infantry and tank forces into that area. With our deception plans in effect we can only hope they continue to believe it. We have used several deception plans in the past, and they worked out to the letter, hopefully the last one will also be effective."

"I agree with that," General Bradley said.

Eisenhower moved to his seat at the table. "As you know gentlemen, a few days ago we had a disaster with the landing exercise. We lost a great number of men, recovered what we could. The loss of over 700 men is unacceptable, but it happened. We also had ten BIGOT's out there, nine are accounted for, one missing, this concerns me. We assume he went down on one of the LST's and if he did, then we are safe. If he survived and the Germans get their hands on him, then we may be in for a hard time."

Montgomery leans back in his chair. "I'd say that would be a sticky wicket old chap."

"Well put Monty. Let's hope for the best."

Eisenhower lights a cigarette and leans back. "That's all for today gentlemen. We will meet back here tomorrow at 0900 hours."

Walker wakes to find Helen in the room sweeping the floor. She noticed he was awake and now sitting up in bed.

"I'm sorry if I woke you," she said.

"That's all right. What time is it anyway?"

"Its 7:10. Did you have a good nights sleep?"

"Yes I did," responds Walker. "You start early I see."

"Well yes, things to do, always things to do."

"I'm sure you keep busy keeping up with the place, animals and all."

"It's not so bad, Fred helps me a lot."

"I want to ask you and don't be offended, but can I trust Fred? I mean would he turn me over to the Germans?'

"Oh no, he wouldn't do that. He comes from a long line of English, he hates the Germans. You don't have to worry about him."

"That's good to know."

"I'll bring you some breakfast shortly. If you need Fred to help you, I'll send for him."

"That would be great."

"I'll go find him right away." She smiles and leaves.

After Fred helped Walker to the bathroom and back to his bed, they made some small talk, and then Fred left.

A few minutes later, Helen came in with a tray of food; She placed it on Walker's lap. There was eggs and ham, home made bread and tea.

"This looks wonderful," Walker said.

Helen moved a chair next to the bed and took an extra cup of tea from the tray.

She sipped the tea as Walker ate.

"I've been wondering about you, John. How is it you ended up in a raft in the channel? I know you said it was a secret, but your secret is safe with me."

Walker finished his food and drank some of his tea, thinking about the question she asked.

"Yes, it is a secret, lets keep it that way."

"You don't trust me?"

"No, it's not that, you have been very kind to me, but you are a civilian and my mission is a military matter."

"Yes, I understand. I may be a civilian, but at one time I was involved with the resistance."

Walker has a stunned look on his face. "You mean like the French Resistance?"

"Well something like that, but not in France, here on the island. At first when the Germans came, there was a group of us decided to form a resistance group. It did not last long, people started escaping to England, and so the group broke apart. Only myself and John Green remain, he lives on the other side of the island."

"That amazing," Walker said. "You in a resistance group, I would never have thought that."

"Oh yes, it is true. I can field strip a Sten Gun and fire one too. I can send Morse Code, in fact I still have a transmitter hidden in my bedroom."

Walker sat straight up in bed. "You have a transmitter? Is it key or voice?"

"Both, but I never used it with voice, only with key. In fact, I only used it a few times before the group broke up."

"Is it still operational?"

"I don't know if the batteries are still good, I have an extra battery."

"Would you check it for me?"

"Sure, I can do that. I'll do it right now."

6

Helen found the secret panel in her bedroom that her father had also built for her safety. She opened it by pressing on a certain place on the wall near her bed. She opened the small door and entered a small room about the size of a walk in closet.

She turned on the light, and took a seat at a roll top desk. She moved the cover back, there is the transmitter, as she had left it years ago. The transmitter had been smuggled in by her father one day, he taught her how to use it after she learned Morse Code. The transmitter is British military, the most powerful one they have.

She turned on the power and waited for the tubes to warm up. The charge indication gauge shows that the battery is weak. She opened the top cover and took out the battery. She pulled out a drawer on the desk and located a battery there. She placed the new battery in the transmitter and turned on the power, the gauge shows full strength.

She decides to test it out. She placed the earphones on her head and turned the frequency dial and immediately found a transmission from some unknown source. It was a voice transmission but she could not understand all of it because it was in German. She turned the set off, shut the door and returned to the secret room.

Helen found Walker up on crutches returning from the bathroom.

"Should you be up walking?"

"Had to go to the bathroom, I didn't want to bother anyone with help."

"You could have pushed the buzzer, I or Fred would come."

"Oh its all right, the ankle feels much better, should be able to walk on it soon."

"Well we'll see about that," Helen said as she helped Walker back to bed.

"The transmitter works, it has full power, had to put the other battery in it."

"That's great, good to hear that," Walker said with a grin. "You still remember your Morse Code?"

"Why do you ask?"

"I want you to send a message to England."

"I think so, but I may be a bit rusty and slow. I can disconnect the key and practice on it for a while, that would be the thing to do. But, sending a message could be dangerous, it may be picked up by the Germans, they have a communication station here."

"I understand that, but you would not send a message in plain language, but in code."

Yes, but the Germans could still triangulate the signal and if they do it right, they can pin point it to here. Of course, if the message is short, they may not have the time to locate the signal."

"You'll do it then?"

"I don't know John. Is the risk worth it?"

"Helen, I need to get off this island and return to England as soon as possible, I can't let the Germans find me. Are there any fishing boats available that can take me, or even a smaller boat I would take a chance in?"

"No, most of the boats are gone when people left here. The few that are left are not sea worthy."

"Then someone needs to come for me, but first they need to know I'm here, and that's were you come in."

"I want to help you John, but I feel its too dangerous, not only for you but for me also. I have heard stories of what they do to women in those concentration camps."

"Come with me and Fred too. You can stay in England until the war is over, and then come back here."

"Do you really believe they will come to get you, you're that important?"

"Yes, I am that important."

She is silent for a few minutes and leans back in her chair. "Why are you so important?"

Walker looks at her for a long minute as if thinking it over in his mind.

"I hope I can trust you."

"You can, believe me John."

"I'm not suppose to tell anyone of what I know, it is top secret but I'm willing to take a chance on you, if it will help getting me out of here."

Helen has a blank look on her face and does not respond.

"There was an exercise for the invasion of France that went all wrong. We got caught by a bunch E-boats and they sank all of our LST's. I was on one of them but was fortunate to escape before it sank. I ended up in the life raft which you found me in."

"What is an LST?"

"It's a landing craft, brings troops in to the beach."

"I see and the reason for not being captured by the Germans other than being a POW is that you don't want them to know about the exercise?"

"No it's more than that Helen. You see I'm a BIGOT."

She laughs out loud. "You're a what?"

"A BIGOT, it's an acronym for British Invasion of German Occupied Territory and a code name for me and a handful of others."

"I've never heard of such a thing," Helen said with a puzzled look.

"Of course you wouldn't, its top secret."

"And what does a BIGOT do?"

"Its not what we do, its what we know.

"Really?"

"You see, I know where the landing site will be in France. The Germans would really like to get hold of someone like me. I was in command of a battalion of engineers to go in and clear the beach of obstacles, so I had to know what kind of beach we would deal with, so I had to know the landing site. There were ten of us BIGOTS involved in the exercise, but I believe I'm the only one who survived, but I'm not sure. There were many men in the water and all of the LSTs sank. So you see Helen, I can't be captured, they have ways of extracting information."

"I see what you mean. I'll help you. I'll send the message."

"Great, your wonderful."

"I'll go and get pencil and paper, you write down the message and I'll code it."

Helen returned ten minutes later with pen and paper. Walker took it and wrote, BIGOT here, need to come home. "That should be short enough."

Helen agreed nodding her head. I'll go and code it, but there might be a problem."

"And what would that be?"

"My code book is over four years old, I don't know if they are still using the same codes and also they may not accept my call sign."

"Hell, that might be a problem," he said. What is your call sign?"

"Bitch Dog," she said smiling.

"Ah, that's a good one."

Helen takes the paper, looks it over a minute, and then turns to leave. "I'll give it a try, that's all I can do."

Fifteen minutes later Helen returned to Walker's room with a gloomy look on her face. He could tell things did not go well. "What's wrong?" He asked.

"I coded the message using my code book, and sent it out with my code name but got no response. I then just sent out my code name, same thing, no response."

"Maybe they didn't get it, transmitter doesn't have the power," Walker said.

"No that's not the problem, it has the power. I'm sure Bletchley Park picked it up, they just didn't answer. You know of Bletchley Park?"

"Yes I'm aware of it, a code breaking listening post which regularly penetrates the secret communications of the Axis powers. But why didn't they not answer your transmission?"

"My guess is that they don't know who I am, my code name is almost four years old, probably don't have me on their list any longer. They probably think I'm some German agent playing around on the airwaves."

"Any other ideas?" Asked Walker.

"When I used the transmitter, I had a certain time for transmission, 1900 hours. I can try again at that time, but each time I get on the air increases the chance the Germans can pick up my transmission. They can't read the message but they have an increased chance to home in on where the signal is coming from."

"It's your call," Walker said.

"I'll try again at 1900 hours."

Walker nods his head and lies back on his pillow.

Later, Helen returned with a tray of food. "Fish and chips and tea for you John. Not actually American food, but quite British as they say."

"Looks good to me."

"We don't have hamburgers here," she said with a grin.

"I have eaten British food before, I've been in England for six months."

"Oh I see. I'm sorry I don't have coffee, it is very hard to come by here."

"That all right, the tea is fine."

She poured him a cup of tea and did the same for herself from the small pot on the tray. "I transmitted again at 1700 hours, but again did not get an answer. I am really afraid to try again."

Walker nods his head as he takes a sip of tea. "It's all right, you tried, that's all I ask of you."

"We will need to come up with a different plan."

"I'll be thinking about that tonight," Walker said as he drank down his tea.

Helen gathers up the tray, and gave him a kiss on the cheek. "Good night John."

He smiled, "Good night Helen."

"Go on in," Margie said. "I'll bring a pot of tea.

"Thank you Margie," Mastermann said as he went to the open door of Ferguson's office.

Ferguson looked up from his paper. "Ah, good morning' to ya John, what brings you out this early?"

" Good morning Brigadier. Late last night I got a call from Matt O'Neal about a strange transmission one of the radio people picked. It appears the transmission was sent from across the channel several times."

"Refresh my memory, who is O'Neal?"

"He is the radio listening people supervisor at Bletchley Park, has top secret clearance."

"I see, and what is strange about the transmission?" Ferguson asked lighting a cigar.

"As he explained, it was in a code they could not decipher. He is still working on it. They got a partial location on the signal, appears near the coast of France. He asked me if I had an agent in that part of world trying to send out a message. I told him, no we did not. At this time we only have two agents working, Garbo and George, and I know where they are, and also they have the proper codes."

"Could be some French resistance group or some German agent playing around on the air waves," Ferguson said.

"Possible I suppose, we'll see if O'Neal comes up with something. At any rate I stopped by this morning on my way to the office to see if you knew anything about it or maybe have some ideas."

"I haven't the foggiest idea John. But do stay for a cup of tea, Margie will bring it in shortly."

Just as magic the door opened, Margie entered with a tray of cups and a pot of tea.

"Now there we are," Ferguson said as he poured the tea. "Meet me at the club later for a drink, said what? Make it around 1400 hours."

"My pleasure Brigadier," Masterman said sipping his tea.

7

Helen and Fred are outside doing the routine chores, Fred hauling hay that he had previously cut, and Helen is feeding the chickens. Helen looks up to see a kublewagen stop next to the barn. There is a driver and a man in the back, an officer as she can tell. The man steps down from the car, she knows this man, Max List, Hauptstrumfuhrer, commanding officer of the German base here.

The man walks up to Helen, takes her hand and moves it near his mouth with a fake kiss. "Fraulein Wilkerson, what a pleasure on this fine morning."

Helen snaps her hand back. "Good morning Hauptstrumfuhrer List," she replied trying to be polite.

"I was just in the area, saw you here and decided to stop and say hello, its been some time since I last saw you, duty calls which does not leave me with time to socialize."

Helen steps back and continues to feed the chickens while List moves to pet one of the horses near the barn. Helen throwing out feed and keeps an eye on List. She mumbles to herself, "What does that Nazi bastard want?"

List moves to the barn and looks in to see Fred stacking hay in the loft. List does not speak but looks around in a sweeping motion. He then quickly moves back to where Helen is standing. "Have a good day Fraulein," gives a half military salute, returns to his car, jumps in and motions for his driver to go.

"Thank goodness," Helen said as she watched the car roar off.

Fred came out from the barn. "What was that all about?"

"I'm not sure Fred. Strange for him to show up like that and then suddenly leave. I get the feeling that he was sniffing around with that nose of his, like he was looking for something."

"But for what Missy?"

"I don't know Fred, you know how the Germans are." She said continuing to throw out chicken feed.

Fred nods his head, "Oh yes, they don't have a reason for the things they do. Well I'm back to my chores. Should have the hay put up shortly."

"You're a good man Fred."

Fred smiles and returns to the barn.

Helen had prepared ham and cheese sandwiches, which she takes to Walker.

"Those look good," Walker said taking one as she pours the tea.

"I thought we would have lunch together."

"I can't think of nothing better," he replied.

"List stopped by this morning, nosing around. Kind of got me worried."

"Who is List, a German?"

"Hauptstrumfuhrer Max List, commanding officer of the base."

"What did he want, did he say?"

"No, just looked around, that's what worries me. He did not just stop by to say hello, he's up to something."

"I hope it's not about me."

"No, I don't think so, but he's one you can't trust. I'll keep my eye out for him."

"How large is the base, how many men would you say?" Walker asked.

"Probably 80 men on base and a 100 or so on the E-boats, they have 10-12 boats.

"The ground people are Army military but List and his adjutant Wolf Kruger are SS, bastards both of them."

"I see you don't have much love for them."

"Ha, if I could shoot them and get away with it, they would be history."

"You know how to shoot?"

"Oh yes, remember I told you how I can handle a Sten gun?"

"Oh yes, that's right. You still have the Sten?"

"Yes I do, and a Luger, both hidden away."

"And ammo, any ammo?"

"I have three full magazines for the Sten and an extra two hundred rounds with the magazine loader. And also a box of 9mm for the Luger"

"I noticed you said magazines instead of clips like most civilians."

"Part of my training John."

He smiles, "My kind of woman."

She returns the smile.

"I'll be back this evening with supper," she said and leaves.

That evening Helen came in with a tray of food. "I made some more stew, I hope you don't mind."

"No not at all, the stew is good," he said sitting up.

"There is enough for both of us, so if it's all right, I'll have my supper with you."

"That's fine by me Helen," he replied.

Helen sits a bowl of stew in her lap and begins to eat. "You know, I've been thinking about sending another message, and hope Bletchley Park can figure it out. What do you think about that?"

Walker rubs his chin and is silent for a moment.

"Could be dangerous if the Germans intercept the same message again," replied Walker. "They might be able to triangulate the signal directly back here."

"I know, but it's worth a try. Let me try one more time."

Walker studies her face for a long moment. "O.K. Helen, go ahead, give it a try, but let it be the last time."

"Sure, after we finish eating, I'll give it a go."

And after supper Helen went to her cubbyhole, turned on the transmitter and worked the key with her coded message again at 1900 hours. She had considered sending it open without code but decided against that as too dangerous.

Later that night she stopped by Walker's room to tell him what she did and to say good night. "I'm sorry John but there was no response to my transmission."

"That's all right Helen, I know you tried and that's all you can do. Better not to send any more transmissions, too dangerous.

Helen smiles and nods her head.

After she left, Walker seemed to be pleased for her effort and was soon asleep.

Masterman was working late at his office when he received a call on his secure phone. Masterman looked at the phone, "Who the devil can that be?"

"Masterman here."

"John my dear fellow, O'Neal here. Just wanted to let you know we picked up that strange signal again in a code that we don't understand. I know you said that you have no agents out there sending any strange codes but I wanted to let you know.

"Well thanks Matt for letting me know. I don't know who that would be except someone who doesn't know what they are doing or some German agent fooling around."

"You're probably right John, we'll keep listening, see where it leads. Probably nothing to it, but worth keeping an eye on. I feel it may be a German agent trying out a new code."

"A possibility Matt, didn't think about that."

"Oh by the way, we got a fix on it with this latest signal. Its coming from an area that seems to be the coast of France, but not on land itself, more like in the water."

"Really? That's interesting. Someone in a boat, maybe?"

"Hard to say John."

"Hold on a minute Matt," Masterman said as he reached for a rolled map of the English Channel. He unrolled it and weighted down the corners with objects on his desk.

"I'm looking at a map of the English Channel," he said into the phone. "I see the Channel Islands are near the French coast. One, Alderney Island is only about ten miles from the coast. Could the signal be coming from there?"

"Hmm, that's a possibility. See what you can find out through your intelligence and we will keep an ear out for any additional signals."

"Yes I will do that. Let me know if you have anything new."

"Of course old chap," then he rang off.

Later the next day in the afternoon Masterman met Ferguson at the club in his usual chair.

"Ah, John my dear boy, take a seat. Care for a brandy?"

"Sounds good to me Brigadier."

Ferguson waves as a passing barman and indicates two brandies.

"What's new with you John?"

"Things as usual, except O'Neal called again last night, said they picked up that strange signal again. They still have no clue who is sending it but they got a partial fix on it, somewhere off the coast of France."

"Off the coast of France you say?"

"Yes sir, strange, is it not. The only thing out there are the Channel Islands."

"Could the signal be coming from one of the islands? Ferguson asked.

"It's possible, I imagine but, who would be sending it, we have no assets on the islands."

"Probably just a prank," Ferguson said lighting a cigar.

"I have the same mind, or maybe a German agent sending out signals to see who will hit on him."

"That's a thought," Ferguson said.

"I've got Garbo working on it, he might come up with something. And O'Neal plans to keep tabs on it and try to get a better fix the next time the signal is sent."

"Those boys over at Bletchley Park do good work," Ferguson said swirling his brandy.

"Yes sir, they do. Well, I must be off, back to work"

Ferguson nods his head and raised his glass. "Have a good day John."

Helen opened the door to Walker's room, stuck her head in and saw that he was asleep. She started to close the door when Walker opened his eyes.

"I'm not asleep, come on in."

"You looked like you were."

"I'm a light sleeper."

"Yes, you would be, military and all that."

"Earlier I tried sending again, but did not get a response, I'm sorry."

"Not your fault Helen, you tried. Let that be your last transmission please, I thought you had stopped with the one before."

"I'm sorry John but I had to try one more time."

"I see, and I know you are trying to help me, but I'll find a way off this island. My ankle is much better, started waking on it in here. Should be good as new in a few more days."

"Well, don't push it John."

"You worry too much Helen."

"I worry about you. Now I believe the bed is in order."

Walked takes her hand in his, "You could stay here for awhile."

Helen is silent for a long moment, smiles and gives Walker a kiss on his cheek.

"Good night John."

After she leaves, Walker lies back on his pillow. Silently he said to himself, "You're stupid, asking her to stay. That was the wrong thing to say. What will she think of me now?"

Thinking of her he slipped off to sleep.

Max List is standing in front of a map of Alderney Island. The row of other men in the room are Oberstrumfuhrer Wolf Kruger, his aide and Kapitan Zu See Hauptmannn Max Klugmann commanding the E-boat force.

"Gentleman, I called you here to be aware of a certain event," List began. "Our radio operators have recently intercepted several radio signals in Morse Code and in code originating from this island using a very strong transmitter, the kind the military use. Someone is sending signals from an unknown location here on this island. We would like to find who it is. There are not that many civilians left, we need to search their homes and it may be necessary to search the vacant houses also, someone may have a transmitter hidden. We don't know what information they are sending, but I would gather it would be information on our E-boat movements and such."

List points to the map on the wall. "Oberstrumfuhrer Kruger, I want you to take every available man and search this island from top to bottom. Look especially for aerials and wire strung out in trees and such."

"As you order, Hauptstrumfuhrer. I will begin immediately." Kruger said.

"Hauptmann Klugmann, you will send some of your forces to patrol the shores around the island, look for any suspicious spaces such as caves and bluffs that can be used to transmit from, even small towers and coils of wire."

"At your orders Hauptstrumfuhrer. It will be done immediately."

"Very well then, this is an important matter. If someone is sending information on our activities, this can be very dangerous to our operations."

List lights a cigarette, looks at each man briefly. "Any questions concerning your duties?"

Both men are silent, waiting for further orders.

"Very well, carry out your orders, you are dismissed."

Within an hour, German troops are crawling all over the island. Some are searching houses, while others look in barns and outhouses; nothing is left unsearched.

Helen is out near the barn feeding the horses when she noticed many troops combing the beach in the distance. She stopped to look for a few minutes, realizing they are looking for something. She gets a strange feeling this could be trouble.

She finished feeding the horses and hurries to the house. She makes her way to the secret room and opens the door. Walker is surprised by her entrance. She has a worried look on her face. "Something wrong?" He asked.

"There are Germans all over the beach, and on the road too. They are looking for something. I'm afraid they must have picked up one of my transmissions, and are looking for the source. I'm sure they will search all the houses."

"Will they come here?" He asked with concern.

"I'm sure they will, I'm no exception."

"That could be a problem."

"Could be John, but you are well hidden and so is the radio, don't worry."

"I'll try not to, but just in case," he pulls the .45 from the drawer at the nightstand. "I'll try not to use this unless I have to and this." He pointed to a small capsule in the open drawer.

"What's that?"

"A pill, I can't be taken alive."

"No John, no, you can't do that," tears are forming.

"If I have no other choice Helen, believe me, it would be the last thing to do."

"Yes, I understand," she replied wiping away a tear. "It won't come to that John. They won't find you, I promise."

"I believe you Helen," he said taking her hand.

"I better go for now, see what they are up to."

"O.K. be careful."

"I will, see you later."

He smiles, she turns and leaves.

Helen returns to the barn where she can see troops continuing to walk the beach. Up the road there is a car coming, she recognizes it as a German Kublewagen with two people in it, a driver and one in back.

They come to a halt near the barn; the driver opens the door for Oberstrumfuhrer Wolf Kruger. She had met him several times, not a bad sort in her opinion, much more of a gentlemen then that bastard List.

Kruger gives a military salute, "Fraulein Wilkerson, how are you?" He said with a nice smile.

"Very well Herr Oberstrumfuhrer." She returned the smile.

"Please, you can call me Wolf. We need not to be so formal."

"As you say, Wolf." Again she smiles.

"I must say, you look more beautiful each time I see you."

The thought in her head said, 'you are a handsome devil aren't you?'

"Ha," she laughs, "You say that all the time, Wolf."

"Ha, but I mean it my dear."

Helen lowers her head to look at the ground, feeling her cheeks flush.

"The reason for my visit is to advise you that we are searching all the homes in this area. The reason I cannot tell you, but there will be troops here shortly to search your property. I hope it will not be an inconvenience for you."

"No not at all Ober…I mean Wolf."

"Then I'll be on my way," he clicks his heels, returns to the car and roars down the road while she stands there shaking her head.

She quickly returns to the house and to the secret room.

"German troops are coming," she said quickly. "They'll be here shortly, don't make any noise, I'll be downstairs."

Walker nods his head, "O.K. be careful."

She bends over, plants a kiss on his cheek and leaves.

8

Helen was seated in the living room when they came, the Germans led by an Unterofficer. "We have orders to search the house, Fraulein Wilkerson," he said in broken English.

She stood up, "Yes of course, I was warned by Oberstrumfuhrer Kruger of your arrival."

The Unteroffizer clicked his heels and nodded. "Of course Fraulein," he said as he motioned for his men to spread out.

"I can show you the house Unteroffizer, if you like."

"That is most kind of you Fraulein."

The men made a quick search of the lower floor as Helen showed them around. Then to the second floor to search the bedrooms and bathroom.

Walker could hear the footsteps; he remained as quiet as a mouse, reaching for his .45, and ready for whatever might happen.

The last room, the master bedroom was next. Helen opened the door and stepped in followed by the men.

She stood near the bed as they searched. Suddenly she noticed a piece of paper on the floor sticking out from where the transmitter is located. The piece of paper is partially under the false door, an unnatural position. If one of them would see it, they surely would investigate.

She quickly moved to the spot and placed her right foot over the piece of paper, hoping no one had seen it. She stood there with hands behind her back, smiling as the men continued their search.

Then it was over. The Unteroffizer clicked his heels. "We are finished Fraulein. Thank you for your patience in this matter."

"You are most welcome," she said forcing a smile, watching the men leave.

In a few minutes they were gone. She picked up the paper, looked at it. A piece from her tablet, must have fallen on the floor the last time she was there, she hadn't noticed it. It was blank which was good, but if found in its position on the floor, could have been a disaster.

She sighed, watching the men drive down the road from an upstairs window. She went to the secret room and entered to find Walker with pistol in hand.

"They are gone John, don't worry, they won't be back."

"I hope I can be as sure."

"If they come back. I'll complain to Oberstrumfuhrer Kruger. That will stop that nonsense."

"Who is Kruger?"

"He is the second in command of the base. He has this thing for me but I can handle him with the twirl of my little finger."

"I am sure you can."

"Now I'm off, back later with supper. I am going to fix you a ham and potato pie, a real British kind of meal."

"Oh, I look forward to it."

She smiled and left out the door.

Two days later Masterman meets with Ferguson in the club.

"There you are John, right on time. I took the liberty of ordering you a brandy," he points to the table.

"Thank you sir, very kind of you."

"Think nothing of it my boy. How is your day today?"

"Busy, we captured two more German agents that came in last night by parachute. The XX committee have them, already working on them to see if they will turn."

"Bloody good show. Any more news on the signals coming from across the channel?"

"No sir, I talked with O'Neal last night. He reported no new signals have been found. It seems whoever it was sent three signals and stopped."

"Sort of odd, what?"

"Exactly my feelings Brigadier. I still believe it's some German agent probably sending out a new code to see what he can fish in."

"Right. What about our friend Garbo?" Asked Ferguson lighting a large cigar.

"I made contact with him last night, he has nothing to report on the signals, but he did say that one of his assets was told by a fisherman who was fishing near the coast of France, drifted near Alderney. The fisherman saw German troops crawling all over the island as if they were looking for something. He was concerned of his safety so he took off."

"That's interesting. What would all that be about?" Ferguson said waving his cigar in a circle. "These are terrific cigars, the PM gave me a box. They are Cuban you know. Care for one?"

"No thank you Brigadier, I'm sure they are good but I prefer my pipe."

"You know John, the Germans are always exercising their troops. It has occurred to me that is probably the cause of the troop movements on Alderney, nothing more. Perhaps a deception plan by the Germans to throw us off. Remember dear boy that we have used a number of deception plans against the Hun."

Masterman lights his pipe, puffs and nods his head.

"A good assumption Brigadier."

"The yanks came up with the Operation Fortitude Plan, there was Fortitude North and South to mislead the German High Command as to the location of the imminent invasion as I recall," Ferguson said puffing on his cigar. "The North operation was designed to mislead the Germans into expecting an invasion of Norway while the South Operation was aimed to counter the likelihood that the Germans would notice invasion preparations in the South of England. The intention was to create the impression that an invasion was aimed at the Pas de Calais."

"They seem to be effective," Masterman replied. "The Germans have moved a large amount of troops to the Pas de Calais area and intelligence tell us that Hitler is keeping 100,000 men in Norway."

"True my boy. But don't forget the deception we came up with last year, Operation Mincemeat, the deception to cover the Allied invasion of Sicily. We obtained a body, a tramp as it where, who had died from eating rat poison. We dressed him as an officer of the Royal Marines, a major as I recall. The XX committee boys planted papers on him that contained correspondence between two British generals, which suggested that the Allies planned to invade Greece and Sardinia. Ha, in one letter there was the mention of the high price of sardines in London. Quite clever of your boys, what? The body was slipped off a submarine near the coast of Spain. Some fisherman found the body and turned it in to the local officials who turned it over to the Germans."

"Yes my committee did a good job with that one, I must say," Masterman said puffing on his pipe.

"Bloody good show my boy, bloody good."

"Thank you Brigadier."

Masterman yawns, stretching his arms.

"One more brandy and I'm off to bed, need an early start in the morning."

"Jolly good my dear boy."

Walker had found that his ankle was healing well; he was now able to walk on it without any pain to speak of. He was up walking when Helen entered with supper.

"Fish and chips tonight John," she said. "I didn't have enough ingredients to make the meat and potato pie as I did the other day." She placed the tray on the table.

"No problem, fish and chips will be just fine." He takes a piece of fish.

"Good fish," Walker said.

"Fred is the fisherman, he goes several times a week."

"Fish from the shore does he?"

"No. He has a small boat but he doesn't go out far. He seems to know where the fish are, always brings in some."

"I use to fish back home, we had a stream running through our place and several ponds stocked with catfish."

"Catfish? What are catfish, they look like a cat?"

He laughed, and then said, "They are called catfish because they have whiskers like a cat. I'm sure they have a scientific name, but we call them catfish."

"Oh I see. Are they good to eat?"

"Very good."

They finish their meal. "Well, I must be off, to bed early, have chores in the morning."

"It was a good meal Helen."

She smiled, took the tray and out the door she went.

Later that night Walker lay back in bed looking at a magazine, not reading any articles, just turning the pages, thinking on how the hell he could get off this damn island. Soon he was fast asleep.

Something stirred in the middle of the night. He opened one eye then the other to see a figure in the dim light from the open door. It was Helen standing there; he could see her figure by the light coming in from the open door.

"Were you asleep?" She said, without thinking it was a dumb question.

"Yes I was," he answered. "Is there something wrong?"

"No, I couldn't sleep. I'm sorry I woke you."

"It's all right," he sat up in the bed. He could see her form through the thin nightgown.

She moved closer and sat on the bed. He moved next to her.

"I've been thinking, maybe I should try sending one more message."

"I don't think that would be wise," he said moving closer so that his head almost touched hers. "The Germans already are aware of strange signals on the island. One more will send them out looking again even harder."

"You're right, I suppose."

"Don't worry Helen, everything will work out."

She smiled and looked down. He raised his hand and brushed her forehead with his fingertips, and slid his fingers into her hair, and ran them through. He swept it all back and left part of it hooked behind her ear, and part of it hanging free. He took his hand away, she said nothing.

He used the other hand, the same way, barely touching her forehead, burying his fingers deep, pushing them through. This time he left his hand where it ended up, which was cupped on the back of her neck. Which was slender and warm. She put her own hand flat on his chest. At first he thought it was a warning. A stop sign. Then it became an exploration. She moved it around, side to side, up and down, and then she slid it in behind his own neck. She pulled down and he pulled up and they kissed, at first tentatively, and then harder.

He moved the straps of her nightgown over her shoulders. They kissed again. Then she stood and let the gown drop. He saw her nakedness in the dim light.

She got back on the bed as he removed his military issued boxer shorts.

Her lips moved against his and she said, "Is this a good idea?"

"Feels pretty good to me," he said.

"Are you sure?"

"My rule of thumb is those kind of questions are best answered afterward."

She pushed him down on the bed and climbed on top. Her arms where behind her, hands holding on to his thighs. She was balancing on a single point, driving all her weight down though it, rocking back and forth, easing side to side, as if chasing the perfect sensation, and finding it, and losing it, and finding it again, and holding on to it, all the way to the breathless end. Which was where he was headed, too. That was for damn sure. No stopping now. He pushed back hard, lifting his hips, floating her up, her feet off the bed, her knees clamping, thrust and counterthrust all in one place.

Afterward he stayed on his back and she snuggled alongside him. He traced patterns on her hip with his fingertip. She said, "So now, answer the questions."

He said, "Yes I think it was a good idea, and yes, I'm sure."

9

Walter Schellenberg found Strumbannfuhrer Rosseman at his usual place at Himmler's office. He jumped to attention as Schellenberg approached. He gave a stiff-arm salute. "Good morning Oberfuhrer," he said.

Schellenberg returned the salute and placed himself in front of Rossemann.

"I received a phone call the Reichsfuhrer wanted to see me." It was more of a statement than a question.

"Of course Oberfuhrer, one minute please." Rossemann opened the door and disappeared. A few minutes later he reappeared. "The Reichsfuhrer will see you now," Rossemann said, opening the door and stood aside.

Schellenberg entered the large office space to find Himmler at his desk working on a pile of papers. He looked up, "Ah, Schellenberg, you got here."

"As soon as possible, since I received the phone call last night. The trip from Munich is very difficult these days with all the people on the roads, many traffic jams."

"Yes, yes, never mind, you are here."

"How may I be of service Reichsfuhrer?"

Himmler rubs his nose and sits back in his chair.

"Rossemann tells me that he has heard rumors of certain activity on one of the Channel Islands. I doubt it is of any importance. What do you know about it?"

"The base at Alderney reports some unusual radio activity on the island, Herr Reichsfuhrer, the source they cannot pinpoint."

"Alderney, where is that located?" Asked Himmler leaning back.

"It is one of the Channel Islands Reichsfuhrer, we captured them shortly after the war started. They were under the control by the British government until we took over. Alderney is the nearest to France, only six and one half kilometers."

"I see," said Himmler. "And what goes on this island?"

"We have an E-boat station there. In fact they were part of the force that caught the Allied landing exercises and destroyed most of it in the process. I reported that information to you earlier."

"Ah, yes I remember that report. There was a great number of men lost I noted, mostly American troops I believe."

"That is correct Reichsfuhrer."

"And what is your concern now that you are here?" Himmler asked glaring in his usual manner.

"It seems there has been radio activity transmitted by someone on the island. The station there has intercepted three-radio signals in code, a code they cannot read. The commander of the base is concerned, he sent out troops to find the source. Most of the English escaped our invasion of the island but a few remain. He feels that the transmissions comes from someone that remains there."

"That would make sense," Himmler said standing. "Who is the commanding officer there?"

"A Hauptstrumfuhrer Max List."

"He is SS, not Kriegsmarine?"

"Yes Reichsfuhrer, he and his executive officer Oberstrumfuhrer Wolf Kruger command a small group of SS men for security of the base. The rest of the personnel are all Kreigsmarine. A OberLeutnant –Su-See Max Klugmann is in command of the E-boats."

"What is your assessment of the situation Oberfuhrer?"

"It is difficult to say Reichsfuhrer. At first we considered scouts in head of an invasion, but why? There is nothing worth there of any importance, only a few E-boats. Then we considered someone playing a trick to confuse the radio operators but again, for what purpose? And if that is so, then how did they get the transmitter? The radio people reported that the transmitter was a powerful one, the kind for military use."

Himmler returns to his desk, rubs his nose. "Then what is your conclusion?"

"I believe that someone or a group are transmitting for the purpose of escape. They are stuck on the island and want to be rescued."

"But who and why Schellenberg?"

"That is the question Reichsfuhrer. It must be someone important that is in urgent need to escape. Perhaps some downed airman or a group washed ashore and find themselves stranded."

"How does that explain the powerful transmitter?" Himmler asked glaring.

"I believe it has been there for sometime," answered Schellenberg, reaching for a cigarette, and then thought the better of it remembering that Himmler detested smoking in his presence.

"An interesting concept," Himmler stated. "Must have been left there by someone that escaped before our forces came in and somehow a person or persons found it, and are trying to use it as a means of escape, in other words, to bring in a rescue force."

"That is a possibility Reichsfuhrer. However, any rescue force would be spotted by the Kriegsmarine and taken care of. That may be why no unusual activity has been seen on the shores."

"Most likely Oberfuhrer."

"At any rate, who ever it is, they must be important, perhaps have important information that would be useful to us, information that they are not allowed to divulge."

"Good observation Schellenberg. Keep working on it, and report to me immediately of any new events."

"I'll send in one of my agents to look around, see what he can find."

"Very well then. Now I must return to my paper work, always too much paper work. You are dismissed."

Schellenberg gives the Nazi salute. "As you order Reichsfuhrer."

Himmler does not respond, looking down at the pile of papers.

Schellenberg marches out the door and nods to Rossemann as he past by.

Outside Schellenberg blew out a sigh of relief, climbed into the back of his staff car and drove off.

Helen came in smiling with a tray of food and a pot of tea. She prepared his plate and poured a cup. She did the same for herself. She smiled and sipped her tea.

They sat at the table and ate in silence. Walker leaned back with his tea. "You make some good food Helen," he said. "A not so easy task in these hard times."

"I am fortunate to have the farm, it provides for Fred and myself. I don't pay Fred for his work, he won't accept it, and I give him food to take home. Sometimes he eats here after his chores. He lives alone in a small house down the road. His wife escaped before the Germans closed all the escape routes, but for some reason he did not get out."

"Most unfortunate for him," Walker stated.

"I suppose, but he is of great help to me, I'm glad to have him. One day when the war is over his wife will return and things will return to normal."

"The sooner the better," Walker said.

"John, I've been thinking. Maybe I should try to send another message. I'll send it at my old transmission time, 1900 hours."

"Oh, I don't know Helen, its too dangerous. The Germans will be listening; they could easily get a fix on the signal using a directional finder to pinpoint the location, right here. They would tear this place apart."

"I feel it's worth the try."

"You sent three times with no response and had the Germans crawling all over the place. I don't think another message would change things."

"What if I got a reply? They could send in a rescue team."

"The team would probably never make it ashore and even if they did, capture is a real possibility."

"I'm afraid you have a point there."

"I may be stuck here until the war is over," Walker said with a smile.

"Is that so bad?" She said returning the smile.

Mastermann entered the club after lunch to find Ferguson in an overstuffed chair enjoying a large cigar and an even larger brandy.

"Good afternoon Brigadier."

"John my boy, good afternoon to you. A most pleasant afternoon I must say."

"You like this place, I see."

"Of course my boy, a nice place to spend the afternoon. What brings you here?"

John takes a seat and lights his pipe.

"I got a call this morning from O'Neal. It seems he was looking in a drawer and found some old codebooks. Looking in one, he noticed a few code letters he had seen lately. He compared the message with the code letters in the book and found they matched. Decoding the message, he came up with, 'BIGOT here, need to come home.'"

"What, what did you say?" Ferguson almost chocking on his cigar.

"He had to repeat it for me also. It seems there is a BIGOT out there sending for help using an old code."

"Bloody hell you say. How would he know to send a message using an old code?"

"O'Neal found several people listed in the code book using the old code, one code name Bitch Dog who had been a resistance fighter on Alderney Island."

"And where the bloody hell is Alderney Island?"

"One of the Channel Islands Brigadier, Alderney the one closest to France."

Ferguson blows out a long stream of smoke and takes a large sip of his drink. "Yes of course, I remember now."

He takes another sip of the drink to finish it off.

"Allow me to understand, we have a BIGOT out there that must be transmitting a message for rescue."

"Except someone is sending the signals for him, Bitch Dog I would assume."

"We need to find out who Bitch Dog is, and that person's location." Ferguson said. "I assume the person would be a female."

"It would appear so," replied Masterman lighting his pipe.

"O'Neal is working on it. He said it would be necessary to pick through old file, may take some time."

Ferguson relights his cigar. "If this is true, and I assume it is, then we need to get the man out of there before the Germans get their hands on him."

"Very true Brigadier. If we can find out who Bitch Dog is and the location, we can find the Yank."

"I suppose I should notify Eisenhower but I better wait until we have all the information and things are confirmed.

"Yes sir, I would think so."

"Well I'm off to see the PM. Keep me informed John."

"Of course I will."

Later in the evening Masterman is working late in his office when the secure phone rings. Masterman looks at it, wondering who could be calling. He picks it up, "Masterman here."

"John old boy, this is O'Neal. I was hoping to catch you there."

"Working late today, just about off to home."

"This won't take long my friend. I found what I believe to be the source of the transmissions from Alderney Island. It seems Bitch Dog is one Helen Wilkerson. She was in a small resistance group there until it fell apart. Her father had smuggled in a British military grade radio for use to contact us with useful information with the code name Bitch Dog. That was four years ago, she only used the radio a few times, and then the group fell apart. There was nothing there to report so we put her on the back shelf as it were."

"That is interesting," Masterman said taking a seat at his desk.

"I thought you might be interested."

"Very much so. Do you have a location on this Helen Wilkerson?"

"She lives in a small village on Corblets Bay, no known name, just Corblets Bay.

She lives in a manor there near the beach, the only two-story structure there. She has lived there all her life with her father and mother, both gone now. Probably one of only a few people still there."

"Wonder how that happened?"

"Probably didn't get out when the others left or didn't want to leave."

"And now she used her old code to contact us, to inform us there is a BIGOT there."

"It appears that way. We have sent several signals at her transmitting time but got no response, probably afraid the Germans will pick it up."

"That's understandable."

"This is incredible news, I'll need to past this on to my boss."

"Yes of course. How is the old man, Ferguson?"

"Just as ever, smoking those large cigars like Churchill and drinking whiskey at home and brandy at the club."

"That's Ferguson all right. I would like to join him at the club but I am never free from this place, a war on you know."

"Yes we all have our duties," Masterman replied.

"Well, say hello to the old bastard for me. If anything else comes up, I'll call. Have a good night old chap."

"And to you, and thank you for the information."

"In the King's service, pip, pip." Then he disconnected.

Masterman hangs up the phone and shakes his head, "O'Neal, typical Irishman."

Masterman checks his watch. "Not that late, better call the Brigadier." He dials the number.

Ferguson in his flat is preparing for bed after having his usual toddy for the body, is sitting at the bedside contemplating having another toddy when the phone rings in the living room. "Who the devil can that be," he said limping to the phone.

He lifts the phone, "Ferguson here, this better be bloody important."

"How are you Brigadier?" The voice in the phone said.

"John my dear boy, I was about in bed."

"Sorry to disturb you Brigadier, but I received some important news from O'Neal a few minutes ago."

"Now important?"

"Very important, could effect the war effort."

"Tell me."

"Better face to face Brigadier."

"That's how it is."

"Yes sir."

"Well you better come over and tell me. I'll put a pot of tea on."

"I'll be there in fifteen minutes."
Ferguson grunts, and then hangs up.

10

Masterman, true to his word, appeared at Ferguson's flat in fifteen minutes.

"Have a seat dear boy," Ferguson said as he poured two cups of tea.

"Now tell me, what is so important that brings you here in this ungodly hour?"

"O'Neal called while I was still at the office with some important news."

"Something new with radio signals they have been monitoring, I assume?"

"You can say that, Brigadier. It appears O'Neal found some old codebooks hidden away in a desk drawer. While looking though one, he remembered some of the code letters looked familiar. Again he matched the code up with the one sent three times. It was a short message that read, BIGOT here, need to come home.

"Is Bletchley Park able to tell where the signals originated? Ferguson asked pouring some more tea.

"They believe it is coming from Alderney Island, one of the Channel Islands. Alderney is nearest France, only ten miles."

"This is most incredible. I will have to notify the PM in the morning."

Masterman lights a pipe, "We also need to let Eisenhower know of the situation."

"Exactly my boy, you can handle that."

"Yes sir, I'll make arrangements to see him."

"Has O'Neal found who sent the messages?"

"Yes sir, a lady who lives there by the code name Bitch Dog, remember as I mentioned before."

"Yes of course. "Bitch Dog is it. What kind of code name is that?"

Masterman shrugged his shoulders. "Who knows Brigadier?"

"Do they know her real name?"

"Helen Wilkerson, she lives at Corblets Bay, in a manor."

"How did she come by the transmitter?"

"Not real clear on that Brigadier. At one time she had been a member of a small resistant group on the island but it fell apart as people left as the Germans took over the island. We can only guess the transmitter may have been dropped by parachute or brought in on a boat."

"My God! Ferguson explained. "If the Germans capture the BIGOT with the information he has, the invasion is in trouble."

"I would image he would not allow himself to be captured Brigadier."

"I see what you mean, dear boy, with the pill those chaps carry. But there is always the outside chance he would not have time to take it."

Masterman nods his head, "A possible thought."

"We need to come up with a plan to get the yank off that bloody island," Ferguson said lighting a cigar.

"That may be a difficult task Brigadier. There is an E-boat base there, Kreigsmarine and support personnel."

"Work on it, my dear boy. Now I'm off to bed, I suggest you do the same."

"Yes Sir, of course.

The following morning Ferguson met with the PM and related the story, which had a great effect on the man. "This is most distressing to think there is a man out there that has the invasion plans," Churchill said.

"I agree sir, a serious situation indeed," Ferguson replied.

"We need a plan to get that fellow back home," Churchill said lighting a large cigar.

"Indeed, Masterman is charged with that one."

"I see, and he is a good man I'm sure."

"The best we have sir."

Churchill leans back, puffs on his cigar. "Has Eisenhower been notified of the situation?"

"Masterman is on his way as we speak."

"Good, lets see what Eisenhower can come up with, he has a good staff."

"I'll report back to you as soon as there is any news."

"Yes, do that Brigadier, by all means. And now you must excuse me, I have a meeting to attend. Always so many bloody meetings."

And with that Ferguson leaves, climbs in the back of his car, slides the glass panel open, "To the club James, I feel a brandy is in order."

James looks into the rear view mirror, put a grin on his face, "Right away guv."

At about the same time, Masterman sat in Eisenhower's outer office, he had made an appointment to see the general earlier. The sergeant at the desk motioned for Masterman, "The general will see you now"

The sergeant opened the door and Masterman went in to find the general at his desk. He made that famous grin, "John Masterman, what a pleasure, take a seat. Coffee, tea?"

"No general I'm fine."

"Well, what brings you out here? I haven't seen you in over a year."

"I'm sorry to disturb you general, I know how busy you are."

"Well you did say it was of importance, so tell me what's on your mind."

"Bletchely Park had received three strange transmissions this past week. They could not decode the messages, because it was an old code. After some searching, the supervisor out there, O'Neal, found an old code book and was able to decode the signal."

"And what did it say?"

"BIGOT here, need to come home."

Eisenhower almost dropped his cigarette. "What? Are you sure that's what it said?"

"Yes sir, according to O'Neal."

"My God, can it be?" Eisenhower said lighting another cigarette.

"Yes sir, hard to believe that there is a BIGOT out there."

"Just where did this transmission come from?"

"Alderney Island sir."

"Alderney Island? That's a Channel Island."

"Yes sir, it is. O'Neal found that at one time there was a small resistant group on the island, and apparently had a transmitter. We think it was a women transmitting, she was in the group for a short time. Her name is Helen Wilkerson. She has lived there all her life and stayed on after most of the people escaped before the Germans moved in."

"That is odd, she must get along with the Germans."

"It would appear so general."

"You say she only transmitted three times. Makes me wonder why she stopped."

"Probability afraid the Germans would pick up her signal."

"Good point, but can we trust her?"

"I don't think we have much of a choice."

"Yeah you're right," Eisenhower said as he poured a cup of coffee. "I'll get my staff together to plan a rescue. If the Germans get hold of him, we're screwed."

"Which BIGOT can it be general?"

"There is only one it can be, Lieutenant Colonel Walker. All the others are accounted for. He must have survived the attack and drifted to that island. It appears that this Helen Wilkerson is hiding him at her place."

"It would appear so general."

"O.K. John, keep me informed of anything new."

"Yes sir, I will."

And with that Masterman left, got in his car and drove off.

He looked at his watch, noted the time and said to himself, "I bet I can catch Ferguson at the club."

Eisenhower speaks into his intercom, "Sergeant, send for Captain Abe, have him report to me as soon as possible."

"Yes sir, right away," a voice answered.

"Ah, there you are my boy, take a seat," Ferguson said swirling his brandy glass.

"I knew I would find you here Brigadier."

"But of course my dear boy. Where else would I be?"

Ferguson waved at a barman and held up two fingers. "How did it go with General Eisenhower?"

"I explained the situation, he is concerned. He will meet with his staff to try to come up with a plan to rescue the man."

"Jolly good, I'm sure they will come up with a workable plan. Ike has a good staff."

"Let's hope so." Replied Masterman.

"Let us finish our drinks and have an early dinner, say what?" Ferguson said looking at his glass.

Masterman looks at his watch, nods his head. "O.K. I can do that."

Captain Abe stands in front of Eisenhower. "Reporting as ordered general."

"At ease captain. A situation has come up of great importance. It could affect our invasion plans. This is strictly top secret captain, do I make myself clear?"

"Yes sir."

"I want you to find me a team of men for a highly secret mission, three or four men should do. Have them report to me, I will disclose the mission at that time."

"Yes sir, I have some men in mind."

"Very well then, return to your duties."

"Yes Sir," Abe saluted and reached for the door.

"And captain," Eisenhower said.

Abe turned, "Sir?"

"Remember this is top secret."

"Yes Sir."

Heinrich Himmler entered his office early as usual. He found Rossemann at his desk near his office. Rossemann stood and saluted as Himmler approached.

Himmer nodded, "Come in Rossemann I have matters to discuss."

Rossemann followed Himmler in and stood in front of his desk. Himmler sat his briefcase on the desk and sat down.

"Rossemann, find Schellenberg for me and give him these written orders." He hands Rossemann a single page of paper. "He must report to me immediately, understood?"

"As you order Reichsfuhrer."

"Very well then, you are dismissed."

Rossemann gave a salute and marched out.

Eisenhower is having coffee and smoking a cigarette when a voice came on the intercom." Captain Abe is here to see you general."

"Send him in."

Captain Abe comes in, salutes.

"At ease captain. What have you got for me?"

"Sir, I have some men outside that I believe will fit your requirements."

"O.K. send them in, and you are dismissed."

Captain Abe opens and motions the men to come in as he leaves.

The men stand at attention in front of Eisenhower.

"At ease men, take a seat. I have a mission to discus with you. This a highly secret mission, so if you want to back out, now is the time to do so."

None of the men move.

"I have your jackets here and see all of you are highly trained. Jump school and Commando training and Rangers. Corporal Waggoner, I see you're trained on radio communications."

"Yes sir, that's correct."

"Very well. Lieutenant Jones, you will be in charge of the team. Along with Lieutenant Jones who is Ranger trained and Sergeant Thomas who is also Ranger trained and Corporal Waggoner will make up the team."

Eisenhower moves to a map tacked on the wall. "This is Alderney Island, one of the Channel Islands. There is a man there that we need to rescue. He has vital information that we do not want the Germans to have. You do not need to know what that information is, but I assure you it is of vital importance. Any questions?"

None of the men respond.

"Very well then. You have three days to prepare for this mission. You will be taken by submarine across the English Channel to a point in Corblets Bay on the Alderney Island. Once in position, you will go in on a raft. There is a point of rock that you can use for guidance. Once ashore, look for a two story building, should only be a few hundred yards off shore. That is the Wilkerson manor. A Helen Wilkerson lives there. We believe that Lieutenant Colonel Walker is there. You will have to identify yourselves. She may think it is trick by the Germans to get Walker."

Eisenhower hands Lieutenant Jones a single piece of paper. "I have written this to help convince her who you are."

Jones nods his head and sticks the piece of paper in his tunic.

"After you have secured the colonel, return to the raft, radio the sub. Then it's just a matter of paddling to the sub and away you go. Any questions, comments?"

The men are silent.

"Very well, get your written orders outside from Captain Abe. You are dismissed and good luck. And remember men, this is top secret."

11

Schellenberg reads the written orders handed to him by Rossemann. "It says here I am to fly to Alderney Island and inspect the base and island. Once there I am to meet with their chief radio operator and survey the island for a radio transmitter."

Schellenberg lights a cigarette, shakes his head. "What the hell do I know about radio functions? They have already searched for the transmitter and found none. The signal has been sent three times and no more. I don't see that I can make a difference. This is a waste of time, my time."

Rossemann remains silent, lights a cigarette.

"But of course, orders from the Reichsfuhrer cannot be dismissed," Schellenberg said, folding the paper.

"I will leave in the morning Rossemann, have a plane ready for me first thing in the morning."

"As you order Oberfuhrer."

After Rosseman leaves, Schellenberg sits at his desk and pours a cup of coffee.

He shakes his head in disbelief and quietly said to himself, "Heni is sending me on a wild goose chase. These Nazis will cause us to lose the war."

The following morning Schellenberg climbed aboard a Ju-52 transport plane and flew off to Alderney Island. The trip was smooth, without incident.

He landed several hours later at the E-boat base and was met by Hauptstrumfuhrer Max List.

"A great pleasure," List said clicking his heels. "This is Oberstrumfuhrer Wolf Kruger, my second in command." He also clicks his heels.

Schellenberg nods his head. He is wearing his military uniform rather than his usual civilian clothes for a greater effect.

"Allow me to show you to your quarters," List said. "It is not far, just up the road. You will stay at the Wilkerson Manor, a very nice place."

"Wilkerson Manor? Is this place under your control?"

"A lady lives there, Helen Wilkerson. She has accommodated many of our guests in the past. She is a very good cook and the rooms are very comfortable. I am sure you will be pleased."

"Then I look forward to it," Schellenberg said with a slight grin.

At the manor Schellenberg is introduced to Helen and taken to his room.

"This is very nice Fraulein Wilkerson," Schellenberg said.

"It is my pleasure, Herr Oberfuhrer. I will serve lunch in the dinning room at noon. Will anyone else be present?"

"No, just myself. Hauptstrumfuhrer List and Oberstrumfuhrer Kruger have duties to perform. As of now I will return with them to the base for an inspection tour. I will return in time for lunch."

Helen smiles, "I would be disappointed if you did not"

Schellenberg nods his head in a slight bow. "Until then Fraulein Wilkerson."

He climbs into the kublewagen with the others and they drive away.

Helen watches as they drove down the road, "Bastards." Then she went inside.

Walker had heard sounds of people moving around in the house. He had moved to a far corner away from the door with his .45 in hand. With all that movement it could only mean one thing, Germans are here looking for him or perhaps the radio. Whatever was to come, he was ready, the capsule with the pill inside was close at hand.

Slowly the door opened, he raised the gun, and then lowered it as he saw Helen's head appear. She came in and closed the door.

"What are you doing in that corner?"

"I heard footsteps, lots of footsteps, Germans I assumed."

"Yes there was, a visitor from Germany will be staying here, I don't know how long. His name is Walter Schellenberg, some big wig, an Oberfuhrer under orders of Himmler himself. He showed me the orders from the great man."

"Good God! He will be staying here?"

"Yes, we need to be very careful. I may not be able to come on a regular basis for awhile."

"I see what you mean. Don't worry, I'll be all right."

"He is gone for now, returning to the base. He'll be back at lunchtime. I have some extra food here in case I won't be able to get back."

"Thank you Helen. Be careful, please."

She smiled, "I will John." She kissed him, opened the secret door and disappeared.

Schellenberg made a quick inspection tour of the base. He really did not know what he was to be looking for, everything seemed in order.

"Very nice, the base is clean and the troops all seem to be alert, a well run establishment," Schellenberg said to List.

"Thank you Oberfuhrer, you are very kind."

"Now if I may use the kubelwagen, I have a lunch date."

"Of course, Oberfuhrer. Will you require a driver?"

"Not necessary, I will drive myself."

"As you wish Oberfuhrer."

"I will return later in the day for an inspection tour of the entire island. I believe your chief radio operator will be available?"

"At your orders Oberfuhrer."

"Excellent," Hauptstrumfuhrer."

He climbs into the kublewagen and drives off.

The short distance to the manor only takes a few minutes. There he is met by Helen, who takes him to the dinning area. She had prepared cold ham slices and cheese with dark bread. Tea in a pot is available.

"This looks very nice Fraulein Wilkerson, nice indeed."

"Enjoy your lunch Oberfuhrer. But please call me Helen."

"Of course, Helen it is then. Will you join me?"

"No, I have things to do, perhaps some other time."

Schellenberg nods his head and starts in on the lunch.

Helen goes to the barn where she meets up with Fred.

"Now is it in there?" Fred asked.

Helen takes Fred by the arm and they move to a corner, she said quietly," The Nazi bastard is having lunch. I made excuses to get away."

"Good Missy, you just stay out here until he leaves."

"I'll need to serve him supper and I won't have an excuse to get away."

"Then you'll have to have supper with him," Fred said.

"I suppose so but I'm uncomfortable about it."

"You can handle yourself Missy."

She smiles and reached out and touched Fred's arm. "You're a good man Fred."

A short while later they hear the kublewagen leave. Helen looks out from the barn to see it drive down the road. She returns to the manor to clear the table, there is a note on the table written in English. It said he would have supper at the base and would return late to stay the night. He added he enjoyed the meal.

She shrugged her shoulders, "I'll make sure I'm asleep when he returns," she said to herself.

After she cleared the table she went to Walker's room. "Just wanted to see if you need anything, "she said.

"No, everything is fine, "Walker replied.

"I can't stay, don't know when the Nazi will return."

"I understand," he said.

"Good night John," she kissed him and left.

She went to bed early but awoke when the kublewagen came to a halt near the front door. A few minutes later she could head footsteps in the room next to hers. She turned on her side. "When will he leave?" She asked herself. Soon she was fast asleep.

In the morning Helen is in the kitchen preparing a pot of tea. She is thinking about laying out some sausage and cheese with dark bread for breakfast when Schellenberg appeared with his overnight bag in hand. "Good morning Fraulein Wilkerson."

Helen smiled, "Good Morning Herr Oberfuhrer."

"I was in my room a few minutes ago and I hear a toilet flush. Do you have a toilet problem?"

"No, that must have been Fred using the second floor toilet, the one downstairs is not working," she replied hoping that he had not used the downstairs one.

"Oh, I see, Fred the handy man. He lives down the road, yes?"

"Yes, that's correct."

"I will not have breakfast, I have a busy schedule today. I'm to inspect the Northern part of the island this morning, a part I did not complete yesterday. I will be here for lunch if that is not too much trouble."

"Not at all Oberfuhrer."

"Good, until then," he said clicked his heels and marched away.

Helen put together a quick breakfast for Walker. She went to his room.

"He's gone for now," she said. "He'll be back for lunch. He was in his room when you must have flushed the toilet. He asked me about it. I told him it was Fred using it."

"Did he believe you?"

"Yes I believe so."

"I thought I heard him leave, but he must have still been there. I thought it was safe to use the toilet."

"That was a close call," Helen said. "He's gone for now but plans on lunch here. I better not stay just in case he decides to return for some unknown reason. You never know about these Nazi swines."

At the base Schellenberg had a quick breakfast with Max List. Afterward Schellenberg was introduced to Feldwebbel Hans Gruber, the senior radio operator.

"The Feldwebel will accompany you Oberfuhrer," List said.

Schellenberg and Gruber climb into a kubelwagen and drive off.

"Just what are we looking for Feldwebel?" Asked Schellenberg.

"Things that appear unusual Herr Oberfuhrer. Mounds in the earth that should not be there, coils of wire, wire on the trees and wire antennas on roof tops."

"Yes," Of course Schellenberg said, "A hidden antenna to find that transmitter that has been sending those strange messages."

"There were only three sent Oberfuhrer, we triangulated the last one near here. Three houses, two empty and the Wilkerson house."

"But you checked all the houses and found nothing."

"Correct Oberfuhrer, we searched the houses but a transmitter could be in one, we just have not found it."

"I suppose that could be," Schellenberg said.

After several hours driving around and finding nothing, they stop at the manor.

"I will leave you Feldwebel, I will be here for lunch. Have the driver pick me up in an hour."

"As you order Oberfuhrer."

Helen was in the dinning room when Schellenberg entered.

"Good afternoon Fraulein Wilkerson," he said with a smile.

"Good afternoon Oberfuhrer," she replied with a forced smile. "Are you ready for lunch Oberfuhrer?"

"Yes I am indeed, I have been thinking about it all day."

"You have completed your tour of the Northern part of the island I assume?"

"Yes I have Fraulein Wilkerson."

"Then you have completed your inspection?"

"Yes, I have decided to leave and go back to Berlin. This trip has been a waste of time except for meeting you, of course."

"You are too kind Oberfuhrer. Right this way, I have lunch on the table."

After lunch Schellenberg sits in the living area smoking a cigarette and drinking a cup of tea. A few minutes of small talk, the kubelwagen arrives.

"It has been a pleasure Fraulein Wilkerson, perhaps we will meet again."

"The pleasure has been all mine Herr Oberfuhrer."

Schellenberg clicks his heels and leaves. Helen waves and smiles as he is driven away.

"Good riddance, you Nazi bastard," and with that she slams the door shut.

A few minutes later she takes a tray of sandwiches to Walker.

"How did it go with the Nazi?" Walker asked taking one of the sandwiches

"He's gone, said he was leaving back to Berlin."

"Well, that's good news."

"Thank goodness," she replied. "Maybe we can relax now, since they did not find the transmitter and I stopped transmitting."

"You have a point there Helen," he said taking a bite out of a sandwich.

"I better go now," she said heading for the door. "I'll be back tonight with supper, Irish stew, it is."

"I can hardly wait," he replied.

She smiled and disappeared out the door.

Schellenberg returned to the base where he met with Hauptstrumfuhrer Max List.

"Find everything to your satisfaction Oberfuhrer?" List asked.

"Yes everything is in order Hauptstrumfuhrer. I will leave now and return to Berlin. Have my plane made ready."

"But you have not inspected the E-boat base and that part of the island Oberfuhrer."

"It is not necessary, everything is in order Hauptstrumfuhrer. I will make my report to Reichsfuhrer Himmler and mention your name, perhaps a promotion is in order."

"Thank you Oberfuhrer, your visit has been a pleasure. I will call the airfield to make your airplane ready."

Schellenberg climbs into the kublewagen as List salutes. "Take me to the airfield," he tells the driver and they drive off.

Schellenberg sits back and lights a cigarette. "I'm glad to get off this stupid little Island."

12

Schellenberg landed at a secondary airfield outside of Berlin. His staff car and driver was waiting for him; the pilot had called for it while still in the air.

He is driven to Gestapo Headquarters; the car goes up the ramp in the rear of the building. There the guards jump to attention and check Schellenberg's papers although they recognize him, they are required to check all who enter, including Himmler himself.

Once inside, Schellenberg is escorted by an SS guard in black uniform to Himmler's outer office where Strumbannfuhrer Rossemann is stationed. Rossemann jumps to attention.

"Oberfuhrer Schellenberg, what a pleasure," he said giving a salute.

"And how are you Rossemann?" Schellenberg replied returning the salute.

"Very well Oberfuhrer. How may I serve you?"

"I wish to see the Reichsfuhrer, if possible."

"Yes, of course. I'll see if he is available."

Rossemann disappears through the large wooden doors. A few moments later he returns and motions for Schellenberg. "He will see you now, be careful, his mood is not good today."

Schellenberg nods, "I'll remember that."

Schellenberg enters the office to find Himmler behind his large oak desk with a large stack of papers. He looks up, "Ah, Schellenberg, you are here."

Schellenberg gives the Nazi salute. "I come to report my findings on the Alderney Island question."

"The Alderney Island question?"

"The strange radio transmissions that were reported coming from there."

"Yes, yes of course. What have you to report?"

"I was there for two days Reichsfuhrer, but I must say there was nothing out of the ordinary. The transmission stopped after three were sent. I traveled the island with the chief radio operator, a Feldwebel Hans Gruber. He explained to me that if the transmission was sent again, they would be able to get a fix on it since they had a general idea from which direction it came from. We inspected the general area where the Feldwebel suspected the signal originated. We found nothing, therefore I return to Berlin to carry out other duties."

"And you found nothing as you say?" Himmler said glaring through his glasses.

"That is correct Reichsfuhrer."

"What is your assessment of all this Oberfuhrer?"

"It is certain that someone has a transmitter or has found one. They or whoever send out a code we cannot read and there is no report of a reply."

"And why did they just send three messages and stop?" Questioned Himmler.

"Concern over begin discovered by the base radio station or perhaps the radio batteries went dead," Schellenberg replied.

"But why send the message in the first place? Can you explain that Schellenberg?"

"That is a question I cannot answer Reichsfuhrer."

Himmler rubs his nose and cleans his glasses. "Keep me informed on the situation, report any new findings. Now you may return to your duties."

"As you order Reichsfuhrer."

Schellenberg gives a quick salute and marches out.

Lieutenant Jones and his men arrive to where the submarine is docked. Jones meets with the captain and presents his orders. A corporal Johnson has been added to the team as a backup radioman.

"Very well lieutenant, I have been briefed on your mission, only myself and the executive officer have knowledge of it."

"Yes sir, I understand," Jones said.

"The chief here will show you to your quarters," the captain said. "I'm afraid the accommodations are not great, we have limited space here."

"We'll be just fine sir."

The men follow the chief to the forward torpedo room where the chief explains how the hammocks work. The men look up in amazement. Sergeant Thomas said, "We sleep over torpedoes?"

"Welcome to the Navy," stated the chief. "Lieutenant you can share the executive officer space, there is a bunk bed there."

"No thanks chief, I'll stay with my men."

"As you wish. Make yourselves comfortable, we get underway in ten minutes."

He smiled as he went through the hatchway.

One of the two torpedo men stationed there came forward, "You guys ever been on a sub?"

None of the men said a word; they just shook their heads.

"Well relax, its not that bad."

Corporal Johnson, the backup radioman was the first to respond, "Yeah well, if you like living in a pipe."

This brings a round of laughter from the two torpedo men.

"Men, you relax and make friends with the navy guys here, I'm going forward to talk with the captain," Jones said.

Jones found the captain in the control tower giving orders to get underway.

"This is where I work, lieutenant, care to join me?" The captain said.

Jones did as directed. The captain hands him a steaming cup of coffee.

"I know your name lieutenant, my name is unimportant, and lets keep it that way."

"Yes, sir, I understand," Jones said taking a sip of coffee. "Wow, this is strong coffee. I thought the Army made strong coffee, but this beats it."

The captain laughs and nods his head. "We have a cook that makes this stuff his way, he's from Louisiana, says its Louisiana coffee. Whatever it is, I can't tell you; it keeps us awake."

Just then the sub moves in a slight rocking motion. The captain gives out some more orders and returns to his coffee.

"How long will it take to reach our destination," Jones asked.

"About two days," replied the captain. "As soon as we reach deeper water, we dive and go the rest of the way underwater, safer that way."

"Underwater?" Jones takes another sip of coffee.

"Don't worry lieutenant, we'll take care of you and your men. We will have chow in a few hours. We have good food on board, the cook is great."

"Thank you sir, but right now I believe I'll take the offer of that bunk."

Jones turns and heads for the open hatch to the executive's quarters.

The chief standing near the captain shakes his head, "Land lover."

For the team, the two days submerged seemed like forever, then came the final hour. The men made ready, checking their gear. They all met with the captain in the control room.

"We will bring the sub to the surface now," the captain said, giving the order to the chief.

As the sub started to the top, the captain shook each man's hand. "Once we are on the surface, a crew will bring out the raft. We will be about 300 hundred meters from shore. After you complete the mission, give the radio call, 'mother goose.' Your call sign is 'little chicks.' Everything clear on that?"

"Yes sir," answered the radioman, corporal Waggner.

"Very well then, Chief of the Boat, take them to the forward hatch. Good luck men."

The men followed the chief to the hatch and waited as the sub reached the surface.

The chief opened the hatch and indicated for the men to go. "Good luck fellows."

The men climbed out on the deck, the boat was rocking gently in a calm sea. A team of men emerged from the mid hatch with the inflatable raft. One of them pulled the inflating device and the raft was pushed overboard and held by ropes. A signal was given for the men to climb in.

The ropes were released and the raft pushed away. The men paddled away as the sub disappeared beneath the waves.

"O.K. men, lets take it nice and easy, "Look out for patrols and any other activity," Jones said.

The men paddle with the incoming tide. "We are in luck," said Sergeant Thomas, "We have the high tide."

Soon the shore came in sight. The raft rode the last few meters on a wave. The raft banked in the soft sand, they all climbed out and dragged the raft further in and found a place they can hide the raft in some foliage. Everything looked good so far, except they did not see the sentry up the beach in the fog, but he saw them.

Jones gathered his men together, "Listen up, that large rock over there is the rally point. Corporal Waggner, you stay here as security, keep an eye on the raft. The rest of us will continue to the manor, which should be several hundred meters in that direction," he points. "Once we get to the manor, Sergeant Thomas and me will enter and find out what the situation is. There is a Helen Wilkerson living there, she is the owner of the place. She should be there by herself. We hope she has the colonel hidden there. Corporal Johnson will provide security outside. If we find the colonel, we return to the rally point, get the raft and radio the sub. Everybody clear?"

Then men all nod their heads, "O.K. then, lets go."

Waggner takes a position hear the rally point, a spot where he can watch over the raft and a good field of view in several directions.

Jones and the men approach the manor after a half hour hike. They gather together.

"Johnson, take a position over there," Jones points to a place near the front door.

"You ready sergeant?"

"Yes sir."

"Follow me, we'll try the front door first."

They reach the door and find it unlocked. "How about that," Jones said.

The house is dark; they use a small flashlight to find their way. They clear the bottom rooms, and then head up the staircase. Several stairs make a creaking sound that alerts Helen. She looks at her watch, three in the morning. What made that sound? Not even Fred gets up that early. She stands from the bed just as the door opens; a light shines on her face. "Who are you?" She asked.

"Don't be afraid, we won't harm you," Jones said holding the light on her.

"Will you get that light out of my face?"

"Sorry," Jones said lowering the light. "We are an American rescue team. We are looking for a Lieutenant Colonel Henry Walker."

"I don't know what you are talking about."

"You are Helen Wilkerson?"

"Yes I am."

"We believe you are hiding the colonel."

"I still don't know what you are talking about."

Helen moves to the near wall and turns on the light. She can see the two men there in their Army combat dress.

Jones comes forward. "Are you alone here?"

"Yes I am, I live here alone."

"Did you not send three coded messages to England?"

Helen did not answer trying to figure out if these guys are for real.

"How do I know you are what you say you are?"

Jones hands her the letter from Eisenhower. She takes it, reads it, than hands it back.

"Most impressive, a letter from the great General Eisenhower."

"He thought it might convince you that we are for real."

"If I sent the messages, how did they translate the transmissions, it was an old code?"

"A man at Bletchely Park found an old code book and found your code name, Bitch Dog," Jones replied.

"My God! You are for real, here to rescue John, I mean Colonel Walker.

"Yes, that is the plan. He is here, right?" Jones stated looking around.

"Yes he is, in a hidden place."

"Well, let's get him," Jones said in an urgent tone.

Helen moved to the secret door, trigger the latch. "I'll go in first," she said moving slowly.

Walker is awake; he heard voices in Helen's bedroom. He moved to the far corner on the other side of the bed, .45 ready in hand.

"John," Helen said softly. "John it's me. There are some American soldiers here to take you home."

"What? Helen what did you say?"

At this point Jones stepped forward. "Colonel Walker, I am Lieutenant Jones. I am here with a team to bring you out."

Helen turns on the light. Walker can see the two men standing there, both grinning.

Walker stands, lowers his handgun. "Well I'll be damned, you guys for real?"

"Yes sir," Jones shakes his hand. "This is Sergeant Thomas. I have two other men, one outside and one on the beach."

"How did you get here?"

"We can come in by submarine sir."

"I assume we go out that way?"

"Yes sir, as soon as we can get you to the beach, we have a raft stashed there. Once we get there we call up the sub, paddle out and away we go."

"I guess the messages got through," Walker said as he accepts the cigarette offered by the sergeant.

"It took them awhile to figure it, used an old codebook," Jones said.

"I see, said Walker. "This is great, I'm really going home," he said taking a long draw on the cigarette. "Haven't had one of these for a long time, lost most of them in the channel. Helen here gave me a few German cigarettes which are terrible."

"I can image you had quite a time out there," Jones said lighting a cigarette for himself.

"You can say that lieutenant. Three days in a life raft can make anyone appreciate the dry land. I was almost a goner when I drifted ashore here. If it had not been for Helen finding me, I would not be here today."

"We appreciate everything you have done Miss Wilkerson," Jones said to Helen.

Helen smiles, "glad to have helped out."

"Got any gear to take colonel?"

"Got this small hand bag, not much in it, a few rations, my .45. I'll just leave it here, except for the .45.

"Ready to move out colonel?"

Walker looks at Helen standing there with tears in her eyes. He embraces her and they kiss. "When the war is over, write me. The address is Wilkerson Manor House."

He smiles, "I plan to do that. Take care Helen."

She turns away as he leaves with the two men. She closed the secret door and moved out in the hallway in time to see them leave out the front door. She started to run down the stairs, catch him and hug him one more time but decided against it. She returned to her room and went back to bed.

13

Walker follows the two men outside where they meet up with Johnson. "This is Corporal Johnson, one of my radiomen," Jones said introducing him.

"A pleasure to meet you colonel."

"I'm glad you came," Walker said.

"Let's move out to the beach," Jones stated.

They reach the barn and move to the backside. There they halt for Jones to get his bearings. He points in the direction from which they came. "We'll go that way. Stay in the tree line until we hit the beach."

They move quickly, but quietly and reach the beach in a short time. They move to the rally point, but do not find Corporal Waggner. "Where the hell is Waggner?" Jones said looking in all directions. "Johnson, radio the sub that we are ready for pick up."

"Yes sir." He takes the hand held radio and speaks, "Mother Goose, Mother Goose, come in." There is static and crackling. He speaks again, "Mother Goose, Mother Goose, come in."

A voice answers, "this is Mother Goose, read you loud and clear, confirm."

Johnson keys the radio, "Mother Goose, the chicks are in the nest. We have the rooster. Repeat, we have the rooster."

"Roger, the chicks are in the nest and you have the rooster, confirm. Roger Mother Goose, out."

"Message received lieutenant. They'll surface shortly."

In the sub, the radioman sticks his head out of his room, which is located next to the control room. "Message captain, the chicks are in the nest, they have the rooster."

"Very well, chief, surface the boat."

"Aye captain, surface the boat."

On shore near the beach the men huddle together.

"Sergeant Thomas go find Waggner and check on the raft." The lieutenant ordered.

"I'll be right back lieutenant."

No more than five minutes later the sergeant returns breathing heavily.

"I found Waggner lieutenant, he's dead near the raft, looks like a knife wound. Someone must have snuck up on him and knifed him."

Jones shakes his head, "This means trouble, there could be an ambush waiting for us. We got to get to the raft and make for the water."

The men stand and run as fast as they can to the raft. They reach the raft and begin pulling it toward the water. Flashes of gunfire erupt from the woods on two sides.

The sub has surfaced and can be seen from the shore in the morning mist. The captain is on the bridge with a pair of powerful binoculars, searching the shore.

The gunfire attached his attention. "Damn, they are getting shot to pieces."

"Lookouts down," he orders. He takes one last look, and then follows the last lookout down into the control room. He slams the hatch shut and locks it down with the wheel.

"They are done for," the captain said. "We have been spotted, they are sure to send them damn E-boats out after us. Chief, dive the boat. Make the depth 60 meters, full speed ahead, lets get the hell out of here."

The first to fall is Jones with multiple wounds to the chest. Next Johnson goes down with a head wound and then Sergeant Thomas is hit in both legs and is hit again in the body as Walker attempts to help him.

Walker now realizes that his chance of taking the raft out by himself is not going to happen. He retreats to the woods and suffers a wound to his left arm doing so. He takes one last look at the beach in time to see the sub go down.

He runs as fast as he can, crashing through the woods. He goes to the ground, listening for movement. He knows they will send out patrols to search for others.

He can hear voices in the distance and decides to crawl toward the manor. Daybreak will come shortly; he needs a place to hide.

It takes him an hour to reach the barn. He looks around, no one there, he goes in and climbs to the loft. He lies back in the hay and examines his wound. "Not bad, only a flesh wound, the bullet only nicked me."

Several hours later there is movement in the barn. Walker slowly peeked over the side and saw Fred scooping chicken feed into a bucket.

"Fred," Walker said softly.

Fred continued to work.

"Fred," Walker said more loudly.

Fred looked around. "What, who?"

"Fred, up here. I'm up here in the loft."

Fred looked up. "Colonel, what are you doing up there?"

"It's a long story. Go find Helen, I need to hide."

"Yes sir colonel, I'll get Missy."

It was a mere five minutes later Helen and Fred appeared. She looked up with a smile, "John, what are you doing here. Something went wrong?"

"Hello Helen, you might say. I've come back for some more of your good cooking."

"Come down from there before someone finds you. You can hide again in the secret room. Come on, hurry."

He climbs down, hugs Helen and they enter the manor by the back door. She looks at his arm, "You're wounded."

"Its nothing, only a scratch."

"Let me be the judge of that," she said.

"I heard some gunfire as I came here this morning," Fred said.

"We got ambushed by the Germans, they were waiting for us. Everyone is dead, I managed to get away."

"I'm glad to see you survived colonel," Fred said. "Now, I'm off to my chores."

"Take care Fred."

"Yes sir, Missy will take care of you."

"Come on John, let's get you to the room. Did anyone follow you?"

"No, I'm sure of that."

They enter Helen's bedroom, she finds the first aid box in the bathroom. She moves to the panel and opened the door to the room. They enter; she closed the door, "Lets have a look at that wound."

He removes his field jacket and tunic. "Its really nothing."

"You be quiet," she said examining the wound. She applied some antiseptic, which had him make a face. She then applied a dressing and padded his face. "Now you lie down there and rest, I'll bring you some food."

"You are too good Helen."

She smiled and disappeared out the door.

"Oberstrumfuhrer Kruger, what have you to report?" Asked Max List.

"It appears a small group of American soldiers landed on the beach, for what purpose has not been determined. It appears they may have been commandos."

"Commandos," List declared. "Why would they come here? We have nothing here that is vital."

"Perhaps they were a scouting party for an invasion, Hauptstrumfuhrer."

"Nonsense, we are a small base. Why invade here?"

"A possibility would be to cross over to France, it is only a short distance."

"A good observation Oberstrumfuhrer. Have you considered this may have something to do with the strange radio signals?"

"I see your point Hauptstrumfuhrer. If it is so, then who ever sent the signals is an important part of the plan."

"An interesting point Oberstrumfuhrer. How many landed?"

"We killed four men Hauptstrumfuhrer. I doubt any others got away. We are searching the entire area as we speak."

"This is a very confusing event," List said lighting a cigarette. "I will send a report to Berlin. Keep searching Oberstrumfuhrer. I assume they came in from the sea?"

"Correct Hauptstrumfuhrer, by submarine. Some of our men reported seeing the submarine before it slipped beneath the waves."

List leans back in his chair. "It is my belief that they came to rescue someone that is here, someone of importance. They would take this person and escape the same way they came in, by submarine."

"An interesting concept Hauptstrumfuhrer. We have searched the island and found nothing. And why would they come for someone of importance? There is no one here of importance."

"I see your point Oberstrumfuhrer, but you were searching for a transmitter. Now go and search for a person, he must be here hiding. Search all the houses including the empty ones, barns and out buildings, look everywhere. This person must be of great importance for the Americans to send a rescue team. I want every available man to begin searching immediately."

"As you order Hauptstrumfuhrer."

Helen entered through the secret door with a tray of food. She sat the tray on the table. "Come have something to eat John."

"What have we here," he said taking a seat.

"I believe this is what they call a English breakfast."

"Wow, look at this, eggs, ham, sausage, bread and butter."

"I knew you would be hungry."

"Yes I am," he said, digging in.

They sat in silence and eat and after Helen poured two cups of tea.

"What happened out there John?"

"We got ambushed, everything went wrong. I'm lucky to get away."

"I am glad you got away, John," she said collecting the dishes.

"I don't guess they'll try a rescue again," he said.

"No, not after what happened," she replied. "You may have to stay here for a long time, until the end of the war. That's not so bad, is it?"

He smiled and stood up. "I could think of worse. The thing now is the Germans have been alerted; they'll be all over the place. I am sure they have come to the conclusion that the team was here to rescue someone, and that someone must be someone important."

"I'm afraid you are right John, so we must be real careful now."

John nods his head and lights a cigarette.

"I'll see you later with supper," Helen said. Then she left out the door with the tray.

In Berlin, Schellenberg receives the report from Hauptstrumfuhrer List describing the action that had happened. He reads it carefully while smoking a cigarette. He speaks into the intercom to his secretary, "Have my car ready in five minutes," he said.

He is in full black uniform of the SS today, due to a function he is required to attend.

Outside, the car is waiting. He climbs into the back and tells his driver to take him to Gestapo Headquarters, a trip he has done many times before, but not an enjoyable one. To visit with Himmler was not one of his most pleasant things to do. "I would rather have a tooth pulled then to meet with Heini," he said to himself. The term Heini had been used by his grade school students, a term he hated and no one dared use it in his presence. It had been known on more than one occasion for someone to end up on the Russian Front for making that mistake.

Schellenberg arrived at the rear ramp, which was used to enter the building by car.

The guards examined his papers as usual and then was escorted to Himmler's outer office. There at his desk is Strumbannfuhrer Rossemann. He comes to attention as Schellenberg approached. "Oberfuhrer Schellenberg," he said standing ramrod straight. "How may I be of service?"

"I would like to see the Reichsfuhrer, I have a report to make."

"Yes of course Oberfuhrer, one moment please."

Rossemann moves through the large oak doors, and then returns in a minute.

"He will see you now Oberfuhrer," Rossemann said holding the door open.

Schellenberg enters and gives a salute. "Good morning Herr Reichsfuhrer."

Himmler looks up from his paper work. "Ah, Schellenberg, you are here. Do you have something to report?"

"Yes Reichsfuhrer, it concerns the Alderney Island situation."

"The Alderney Island situation?"

"Yes, I was to report if any changes occur on the island."

"Yes, yes, the strange radio messages I seem to remember."

"Yes Reichsfuhrer that is correct."

"What have you to report?"

"Yesterday, it seems a small American team landed and went inland to some unknown point. A sentry saw them land and notified the base. They came in on a submarine, which the sentry also noticed. When the team returned to the beach, our troops were waiting, all were killed. It appears the submarine was waiting, but after gunfire took place, it submerged and made its escape."

"What was the purpose of this raid, commandos?" Asked Himmler.

"It is not clear what their intentions were Reichsfuhrer."

"How many men came ashore?"

"They counted four killed Reichsfuhrer. We believe that it was a four man team."

"I find that strange Oberfuhrer."

"I believe it has something to do with the radio signals," Schellenberg said reaching for a cigarette, but then thought the better of it because Himmler detested smoking in his presence.

"What do you mean Oberfuhrer?"

"To me it means they came to rescue who sent the radio signals. Someone on the island needs to be rescued."

"An American I assume, since the team was American." Himmler added.

"It must be someone of importance Reichsfuhrer, to send a team in by submarine."

"That would be obvious Oberfuhrer. I am concerned that there appears to be an American or perhaps someone of importance on that island. What is he doing there, for what purpose? Find him Schellenberg."

"All available men are searching the island Reichsfuhrer."

"I will order another fifty men to help with the search," Himmler said cleaning his glasses. This concerns me greatly. Why is a lone American as we suspect, on that island? How and why did he get there, to spy? There is nothing there but a small E-boat base."

"I have a theory Reichsfuhrer."

"Yes, yes."

"If you recall, the Americans and British got trapped in landing crafts by our E-boats two weeks ago. It appears they were in the middle of a landing exercise when the E-boats appeared, probably an exercise for the invasion. The E-boats sunk all the crafts, many men lost, those survived were rescued by the British Navy. We can assume one or perhaps more of the surviving men made it to Alderney Island. One of them is the one who sent the radio messages resulting in the rescue attempt."

"Then one had a radio with him?" Himmler questioned.

"We don't think so Reichsfuhrer, the transmitter would be much too large to carry. There must be a transmitter on the island that he used or someone sent the signals."

Himmler rubs his nose. "Which means someone on that island is helping who ever is hiding, proving shelter and food."

"Exactly my thought Reichsfuhrer.

"He must be someone important, a high ranking officer perhaps,' Himmler said.

"A possibility Reichsfuhrer."

"Then we must find him Oberfuhrer."

"We will find him Reichsfuhrer."

"Good then. Now I must return to my paper work. You are dismissed."

Schellenberg gives a salute and marches out the door. He finds his car waiting in the parking lot near the ramp. He walks over and climbs in the back. He light a cigarette and leans forward. "To the nearest Hofbrauhaus Hans, I need a drink."

The driver nods his head and they drive away.

14

General Eisenhower is busy at his desk preparing for a staff meeting. The voice on the intercom said, "Captain Abe is here to see you general."

"Send him in," Eisenhower replied.

Captain Abe marched in, saluted, "Captain Abe reporting sir.

"At ease captain," Eisenhower said, returning the salute.

"What's on your mind captain?"

"I'm afraid there is bad news general."

"Well, let's have it."

"The rescue team we sent in ran into a shit storm general."

"Tell me about it."

"They managed to get the BIGOT but got hit at the beach, all were killed."

"Including the BIGOT?" Asked Eisenhower.

"We don't know general. The sub reported gunfire on the beach; they got out of there. The captain assumed all were killed."

Eisenhower lit a cigarette, disappointment on his face. "That is most distressing captain. But we are not certain that the BIGOT was also killed?"

"That's correct general."

"Lets assume he is still alive, which means he is a liability."

"Any suggestions general?"

"I'll give a call to our British MI-5 boys, maybe they can come up with some plan."

"Yes sir, what are my orders?"

"Stand down for now captain. I'll let you know of any new orders."

"Yes sir."

"You are dismissed."

"Good morning Margie, the boss in?" Masterman said as he entered the office.

"Go on in. He's reading the newspaper. I'll bring in some tea."

"Thank you Margie." He opened the door and went in to find Ferguson at his desk reading the daily paper.

Ferguson looks up, "John my boy, what a surprise. Have a seat. What brings you out this fine morning?"

Before he can answer, Margie brings in a tray with cups and a pot of tea. She sits it down at the sidebar. "Thank you Margie," Ferguson.

She smiled and went out the door closing it behind her.

"Good old girl," Ferguson said as he poured two cups of tea. He handed one over.

Mastermann takes the cup, "Thank you sir. I came to tell you that I got a call from Eisenhower's headquarters this morning, a very disturbing call I might add."

"Yes, go on."

"It seems the rescue team failed in their mission."

"Any details?"

"It seems they were returning to the beach when they were ambushed, all killed sir.

"Most distressing news, John. All killed you say, including the BIGOT?"

"We don't know sir, but it is assumed so."

Ferguson lights a cigar, puffs a few seconds. "If it is true then there is no need to worry about the Germans getting their hands on him."

"True Brigadier, but what if he is still alive?"

"Then we have another problem," replied Ferguson.

"Eisenhower has asked us for help. To see what we can do." Masterman said.

"Bloody hell, what can we do?" Ferguson replied.

"I'll get Garbo on it sir. Perhaps he can find out something."

"Ah, yes Garbo is it? Can we really trust him? At one time I remember he had been a German agent."

"He played both sides for some time Brigadier. I convinced him otherwise with threats of hanging if he didn't leave the Germans. He agreed to my proposal. The Germans, however, still think he is working for them. We feed the German intelligence, false information, as it were."

"Then I say, see what he can find out," Ferguson said. "Another cup of tea?"

"No thank you Brigadier, need to run. I have a busy day at the office."

"Of course my boy. How about lunch at the club?"

"Yes, I'll see you later."

Several hours later Masterman is summoned to the radio room. Ray Osborn waves at him as he enters. "Hello Ray, what you got?"

"A message from Garbo."

"That was quick."

Osborn hands the one sheet message over. "O.K. lets see what it says."

He reads it out loud quietly. "Intercept from Aldereny Island to German Intelligence, Berlin.

Message reads: A four-man commando team landed by raft from submarine, mission unknown. Five men returned to beach, ambushed by island defense troops, four men killed, one uncounted for. End of message."

"Thank you Ray, keep up the good work."

Ray smiles and returns to his radio.

Masterman returned to his desk and immediately called Ferguson's office. Margie answered, "No, the Brigadier went to lunch. I bet you can find him in the Gentleman's Club."

"Thank you Margie, I'll go there."

Masterman arrived at the Club to find Ferguson in his favorite chair with a brandy in one hand and a large cigar in the other.

"John my boy, what brings you here? A bit early for lunch. Take a seat."

"Margie told me you were here."

"Ha, and where else would I be? What's on your mind my boy?"

"I just received a message from Garbo. He intercepted a signal from Alderney Island to German Intelligence in Berlin. It stated they killed four commandos that came ashore. It also stated there was a fifth man that has not been found."

"He got away?" Ferguson asked.

"A possibility Brigadier, or they just have not found the body yet. I am sure they are searching."

"Could it be the BIGOT?"

"Could be, but there is no way to be certain."

Ferguson blows out a long stream of smoke. "If he is still alive, it doesn't seem another rescue attempt is possible, he may be there for the duration."

"I see your point Brigadier."

"A sticky wicket my boy," Ferguson said swirling his glass. "A brandy?"

Helen returned with supper, they eat in silence. "I've been thinking about sending out another signal. They have my code now, so that won't be a problem."

"It's too dangerous Helen. The Germans are bound to locate the transmission and trace it here."

"I'll move the transmitter to a cave three miles from here. The cave is well hidden, I know it well, played in it when I was a child."

Walker rubs his chin, "That might work but I still think its too dangerous."

"Fred will take it up to the cave in the cart and I'll follow later to transmit."

"I don't know Helen, you're taking a great risk."

"I'll send the same message as before. At least they'll know you are still alive."

"I don't believe they'll send another rescue team."

"That may be so, but at least they'll know you are still here. They might come up with some workable plan."

Walker is silent, thinking and pacing the floor. "O.K. do it but be careful."

She smiles and gives him a kiss on the cheek. "I'll have Fred move the transmitter right away. I'll go up there early in the morning."

Walker nods his head as Helen leaves with the supper tray. "See you later John."

Walker was already asleep when Helen returned and slipped into his bed. "What time is it? I thought you had already gone to the cave."

"There is still time."

At 3'oclock Helen slipped out of the room, Walker was fast asleep.

She went to the barn and saddled up her favorite horse and rode off. She rode along the shoreline but stayed in the trees for cover. She came upon a German patrol walking on the beach. She hid in the bushes until they were gone.

She urged the horse to cantor and covered the rest of distance to the cave in no time.

She found the transmitter set up with the aerials out ready to transmit.

She powered it up, took the key and transmitted in code; "Bitch Dog here, I have BIGOT here, needs to come home."

She repeated it one more time then shut down. She covered the entrance to the cave with some foliage, got on the horse, and galloped away, returning the way she came back to the barn. She put the saddle up and began brushing him down when Fred appeared. "I'll do that Missy, you must be tired, get some sleep."

"Thank you Fred, I plan to do just that."

Masterman arrived at his office on Baker Street at his usual time. As soon as he walked in the door, his secretary handed him the phone. "Matt O'Neal at Bletchley Park on the line for you sir."

Masterman put his briefcase down and took the phone. "Masterman here."

"John old boy, it's Matt."

"What can I do for you Matt?"

"Just thought you would want to know that we received a message from Bitch Dog.

It appears our man is still there, alive and kicking."

"My Lord, can it be true?"

"I would bet my pension on it, old chap."

"I had better let the Brigadier know right away.

"You do that old man, and tell the Brigadier he still owes me a dinner, he'll know what I mean."

"Thanks for the information Matt."

"Anytime old boy."

Masterman arrived at Ferguson's office within ten minutes. "Is the old man in?" He asked Margie. "I need to see him right away."

"I heard that" a voice said through the open door.

Margie smiled, "Go on in John."

Masterman entered to find Ferguson at his desk with a cup of tea and the daily newspaper.

"Old man indeed."

"Sorry sir, I meant no offense."

"Well, take a seat, a cup of tea."

Masterman waved him off. "No thank you. I come to tell you a most interesting fact. I received a call from O'Neal at Bletchley Park."

"And what did he have to say."

Masterman related the information O'Neal had told him.

"My word. The BIGOT is still alive, bloody hell you say?"

"That's my understanding sir."

"I'll need to let Eisenhower know," Ferguson said pouring a cup of tea.

Masterman lit his pipe, took a few puffs. "I was thinking of the problem on my way over here, and I believe there is a solution."

"And what might that be?"

"Well sir, we have an agent that we used several times to impersonate a German officer. His name is Franz Zweiler, born in Germany of a German father and a British mother. He and his mother escaped Nazi Germany before the war started. The father stayed, a pilot killed in the Battle of Britain. Franz is fluent in German, French and Spanish and totally committed to our cause. Once he managed to infiltrate Rommel's staff in Africa to find out certain battle plans. However, before he could complete his task, Rommel returned to Germany.

"And what is the plan?"

"We send him in as a high ranking officer, locate the BIGOT and bring him out."

"You make it sound simple my boy. Tell me more."

"We can put him in a nice black SS uniform with the rank of Standerenfuhrer, that is colonel to us. We'll add the cuff title of RFSS, Himmler's personal staff for an added effect. Add a fake written letter from Himmler, that he is there to inspect the base, and no one will question his authority."

"How does our man get there?"

"He can fly just about anything we have, and also the German aircraft. We have a base named Cold Harbor on the coast north of here. There we keep several captured German planes. He takes one; flies below radar across the channel, then makes a turn over the French coast to make it look like he came in from that direction. He lands at the base, presents his papers, the troops there will fall over themselves to carry out his orders."

"How will he find the BIGOT?"

"We know a Helen Wilkerson has a manor near the base. In the past high-ranking officers visiting the base have been quartered there. We hope this will happen with our man. I suspect Helen Wilkerson to be Bitch Dog, she probably sent the messages. I also believe she may be hiding our BIGOT, or knows where he is."

"You are assuming a lot, my boy. I hope you are correct."

"We have good intell Brigadier. Garbo has sent a lot of information he has gather intercepting their signals."

"I see, then when do you plan on this adventure?"

"Right away Brigadier. I'll get in touch with Zweiler at once and have him meet me at Cold Harbor."

Ferguson leans back in his chair, lights a cigar. "A bloody good plan John, damn good. I approve it completely. Now, I will leave you to your work and call our friend Eisenhower to tell him we have a plan."

"Yes sir, I'll be on my way."

Once back at his office, Masterman called Franz Zweiler and asked him to meet at Cold Harbor this afternoon. He agreed to the meeting since it sounded important.

Masterman left immediately; since he had further to go than Zweiler.

Helen came in with a tray of sandwiches. "How about some lunch John?"

He sat up in bed. "Yeah, sure, I must have dozed off."

They sat at the table and ate in silence.

Walker had finished the last of his sandwich. "You know I've been thinking, maybe I could highjack a plane at the base and force the pilot to fly to England."

Helen looked at him and was at a lost for words for a moment. "Are you crazy? You would never get on the base, and to force a pilot to take you to England is out of the question. The pilot would fly you to a base in France and that's the end of you. It's a silly idea John."

"I suppose your right. I just feel so trapped here. I know the invasion is coming soon and I'm going to miss out. I want to get back into the fight."

"I know, and I understand, but you have no choice right now."

"I know Helen, I'm just blowing off steam."

Helen smiles, takes up the tray, and heads for the door. She stops and turns, "I'll be back tonight to help you blow off some of that steam." She smiled again and went out the door.

Walker shook his head and laid on the bed, "What a girl."

15

After a two-hour drive, Masterman arrived at Cold Harbor. Franz Zweiler was waiting for him in the lounge area. "Hello Franz, been waiting long?" Masterman said shaking his hand. "Only about a half hour."

"Let's get down to business," Masterman said, lighting his pipe.

"What you have in mind, John?"

"I have a mission for you, one right up your alley."

"Tell me."

"I want you to impersonate a German officer, Standerenfuhrer in fact. I know you are good at that, and rather enjoy yourself in that role."

"Yes, you are right."

"You can fly a Fieseler Storch, I assume?"

"Sure, no problem."

"Tomorrow morning, I want you to fly to Alderney Island, Corblets Bay to be exact, there is an E-boat base there. Your mission is to rescue a Lieutenant Colonel Walker that we believe is hiding in a manor owned by a Helen Wilkerson, an English girl. We believe she has him hidden there, or knows where he is. You need to get him out of there, and bring him back here."

"Does the lady know I'm coming?"

"No, you will have to convince her."

"That may not be easy for me in a Nazi SS uniform."

"I have a letter here from General Eisenhower that will help."

"I see a problem, to get him to the plane." Zweiler said looking at the letter.

"That could be a problem, but I'm sure you can figure something out."

"Is there land near the manor?" Zweiler ask.

"She has 100 acres. Maybe you can land near by."

"I can check it out when I fly in."

"Be sure you come in from the direction of France."

"No problem John."

"Here is a letter from Himmler, fake of course. This gives you the authority to make an inspection of the island, no questions asked."

"They will jump to attention when I present that," Franz said smiling.

"I am sure you will quarter in the manor, most high ranking officers stay there from the information I got. Take advantage of that."

"I will. This is going to be good."

"I see you are already enjoying yourself."

"But of course John, I was born for this."

Masterman relights his pipe, smiles, "See you in the morning Franz."

The following morning Masterman met with Zweiler, standing next to a Fieseler Fi 156 in his black SS uniform. On his uniform is the RFSS cult title, the Iron Cross 1st Class on his left pocket, a wound badge is added next to the cross. Above the pocket is the Close Combat clasp and to top it off, at his neck hangs the Knights Cross with Oak Leaves and Swords.

Masterman looks him up and down, "That should bring the fear of God in them."

"Want to play the part," Zweiler said.

"Well, you certainly look it," Masterman replied. "Everything ready?"

"I'm ready," Zweiler said as he climbed aboard the plane.

"Good luck." Masterman said waving.

The engine started, then he taxied down to the end of the runway, turned into the wind. The power was increased, then the little plane roared down the runway and lifted off.

Masterman stood there watching it as it got smaller and smaller and the he returned to his car and drove off. He lit his pipe and shook his head. "That is one crazy son-of-a bitch."

In an hour, the plane crossed the channel flying low to avoid the radar. Then Zweiler crossed into France and gained altitude. He made radio contact with the base on Alderney Island stating the fact that he is Standerenfuhrer Franz Zweiler flying in a Fieseler Storch and would land at the airfield.

Permission was granted and the plane crossed the short distance from France to the island. Zweiler made his approach and made a perfect landing. He taxied to the nearest hanger and shut off.

List and Klugmann are there to meet him. Zweiler got out and walked over to the two men. They saluted, he returned the salute.

"How may we help you, Standerenfuhrer?" List said standing ramrod straight taking in the uniform and Knights Cross.

Zweiler hands him the fake letter from Himmler. "I am here to make an inspection of the island. There have been reports the Reichesfuhrer is concerned about."

"Yes of course, Standerenfuhrer, we are at your command. I am Hauptstrumfuhrer List and this is my adjutant, Oberstrumfuhrer Wolf Kruger."

Zweiler nods his head. "I will require quarters and a kubelwagen."

"You will be quartered at the manor up the road. It is owned by an English woman. The accommodations are quite satisfactory."

"An English women you say."

"A Helen Wilkerson is her name. She stayed on after we invaded. We have no problem with her; she has been very helpful for us. Many of our visitors have been quartered there. She is an excellent cook."

"Then I look forward to my stay."

"When does the Standerenfuhrer wish to start the inspection?"

"In the morning will be acceptable. Now I wish to check into my quarters, have a meal and rest."

"As you wish Standerenfuhrer," List said as he motioned the driver to bring the kubelwagen.

"The driver will take you to the manor immediately Standerenfuhrer," List said.

"What time will you wish to start your inspection Standerenfuhrer?"

"Have the driver come for me at 0900 hours."

"As you order Standerenfuhrer," List said as they climbed into the kublewagen.

They arrived at the manor, Helen had seen them come up the road, and she was waiting at the front. List and Zweiler get out. List salutes, "Fraulein Wilkerson, may I present Standerenfuhrer Zweiler, he will be staying here for a few days."

Helen gives a half smile and extends her hand. Zweiler clicks his heels and takes her hand to his lips. "A pleasure, I am sure," he said.

"Please come in, I will show you to your room," Helen said opening the door.

"You are welcome to come in Hauptstrumfuhrer."

"I am afraid I must return to my duties Fraulein Wilkerson," List said as he returns to the kubelwagen. "The diver will return for you as ordered, 0900 hours Standerenfuhrer."

Zweiler nods his head and follows Helen into the manor. She takes him upstairs to a bedroom next to hers. The room is small but adequate with a large bed, a chest of drawers, a closet and a table with two chairs. "There is a bath room down the hall,"

Helen said pointing.

"This is very satisfactory Fraulein Wilkerson."

"Please call me Helen," she said smiling.

"As you wish."

"I will serve lunch in one hour, in the dinning room."

"I look forward it."

Helen turns and leaves. Zweiler unpacked his small bag and laid things out on top of the dresser. He sits on the bed, lights a cigarette, his mind is going over the plan he has of using the meadow south of the manor to land on. He noticed it when he flew over the manor on his approach to the airfield.

Back at the base List and Kruger are having coffee. List said, "I have never heard of this Standerenfuhrer. "It just seems strange to me that he would show up with an inspection tour, when we have combed the island from top to bottom," List said.

"It appears Himmler sent him to follow up on the radio signals we discovered, and the commando team we killed the other day." Kruger said lighting a cigarette. "He has a letter from Reichsfuhrer Himmler and is on his staff as we can see from his uniform."

"Yes I know," replied List. "But I am still uneasy about this matter. I want you to send a radiogram to an Oberstrumbandfuhrer Waggner in Berlin. He is a friend of mine; we go back to the early days. Ask him to see what he can find out about our Standerenfuhrer Zweiler."

"Yes as you order Hauptstrumfuhrer, right away."

At lunch Zweiler and Helen make small talk. Over coffee, Zweiler revels to Helen how he is here to inspect the island. "There seems to be strange radio signals from here," he said.

Helen is silent and sips her coffee.

Zweiler puts down his cup. "What I am about to tell you, will surprise you, but make no mistake, it is true."

Helen looks puzzled but does not respond.

"My name is Franz Zweiler," he begins. "I am not a Standerenfuhfer. I am an agent working with MI-5 in England. I am here to find Lieutenant Colonel Walker and take him home."

Helen's mouth drops open in disbelief. "What did you say?"

"I am here to take the colonel home. I plan to fly him out in the Fieseler Storch that I flew in here."

"I don't believe you, this is some kind of trick."

"No, believe me. How would I know of Colonel Walker? Bletchley Park received your last message. You are Bitch Dog are you not?"

Helen nods her head yes. "Then this must be true."

Zweiler hands her the letter from Eisenhower, "This will help convince you this is for real."

Helen reads the letter, "Yes I believe you, it must be true."

"Where is the colonel?"

"He is here, hidden in a secret room."

"May I see him?"

"Follow me," she said and they went upstairs to her bedroom. There she opened the secret door. "Wait here, I'll go in first."

She entered to find Walker sitting on the bed. "Helen, what a surprise, is it lunch time?"

"John, there is someone here to help you. Don't be surprised, he is not what he appears to be."

Helen motions for Zweiler to come in. He steps in; Walker cannot believe what he is seeing. A man in a black SS Nazi uniform standing there. Walker grabbed his .45.

Helen came forward waving her hands, "No John, don't shoot, he is here to help you escape, put the gun away."

"That's right colonel, she is correct."

Zweiler tells Walker his mission in detail. Walker, finally convinced, lays the .45 aside.

"This is incredible, totally incredible," Walker said. "When do you plan to pull this off?"

"I am to make an inspection of the island in the morning, that will take all day. I will then make my excuses to List and assure him everything is in order. I will then take off, circle the island and come in and land on the south meadow, it has a nice clear field. Be at the end of the field at 1700 hours."

Walker nods his head, "We can do that, get there on horseback."

"Good, sounds good."

Zweiler looks at Helen, "I'm sorry, but I can't take you, the plane can only handle two people."

"I'll be all right, the Germans won't suspect anything. John will be gone, they won't even know that he was here."

"A brave lady, here colonel."

"Yes she is."

"Then we are good to go?" Asked Zweiler.

"I'm ready." Replied Walker.

"I'll be back with lunch," Helen said. Then she and Zweiler left the room.

Walker lay on the bed, "Damn, I'm finally going home."

The day went by as normal. Helen showed Zweiler the barn and the animals.

They took two horses and rode down the south pasture. They pulled in their horses where Zweiler indicated.

"This is perfect, right here. Be here at 1700 hours. I'll land and turn the plane around for take off. The colonel gets in and we take off."

"Well, that's good to know," Helen said turning her horse.

Helen served Walker his meal and had mentioned she might slip in later tonight, which brought a grin to his face.

Zweiler and Helen eat supper in silence. Later they retired to the living room, had coffee and small talk. Both retired to their rooms early. Later in the night, Helen kept her promise; she slipped into the secret room.

In the morning Helen served breakfast to Walker and Zweiler, they eat together in the secret room. Zweiler told Walker he would see him later in the day. Walker nodded his head and gave Zweiler a simple salute.

Zweiler took his leave, stood outside as the kublewagen came on time.

He rode to the base, met with Oberstrumfuhrer Kruger who is assigned to accompany Zweiler on his inspection tour.

Zweiler and Kruger inspected the north of the island, which took up most of the morning. They returned to the base for lunch, and then headed out for the southern part of the island.

On the return trip Zweiler stopped at the manor to collect his bag and said his farewell to Helen. "Remember 1700 hours," he said. She smiled as they drove away.

Back at the base, Zweiler reported to List that everything was in order and that he would now take off, return to Berlin and make his report to Himmler.

List was more than pleased as he waved when Zweiler took the little plane to the air.

"Come Wolf," List said, "Lets go get a schnapps."

"I got a report back from Berlin Hauptstrumfuhrer as I was on my way here."

"And what did it say?" List asked.

"Oberstrumbandfuhrer Waggner has never heard of Standenerfuhrer Zweiler and there is no record of him on Reichsfuhrer Himmler's staff."

List light a cigarette, "Interesting. Well no matter, he is gone. Probably one of Himmler's little tricks to see how we would react."

"Of course Hauptstrumfuhrer, exactly."

Zweiler gained altitude and headed out toward France to make it look as he was in the proper direction. He kept under the radar, made a turn and came back in toward the island.

He found the pasture with no problem. He made one pass low; he can see the horses and two figures near the tree line. He banked, made the turn and landed on the grass without any problems. He turned the plane around to be ready to take off into the wind, the prop turning.

Helen and Walker appeared, Zweiler opened the door. "Come on, let's go."

Walker hugged and kissed Helen.

"Take care John."

"I will, and you too. I wish you could go.

"I'll be all right," she kissed him again.

"I'll see you after the war," he said.

"You promise?"

"I do." And with that he climbed aboard in the seat behind Zweiler.

The door was shut, power applied, then the plane took off down the pasture and into the air. Helen waved as the plane flew over. She mounted her horse and led the other one back to the barn. She unsaddled the horses, stood in the barn for a moment thinking if she would ever see Walker again.

The flight was uneventful, no British aircraft seen, nor any German ones. They crossed the English Channel and landed at Cold Harbor.

Masterman and Captain Abe were there to greet him. Captain Abe took charge, rushed Walker away to a waiting car.

Masterman went to his car, and drove off to make his report to Ferguson.

The next day Masterman reported to Ferguson with all the details.

"Bloody good show. This Zweiler fellow deserves a medal I should say."

"We don't give our agents medals, you know. We would have to explain what the decoration was for, what deed."

"Yes, I know about all that my boy. It just seems he should be rewarded some now. A bloody good show indeed."

"His reward is playing the part Brigadier. All the reward he needs."

"Indeed, the fellow seems to enjoy himself. Perhaps he should become an actor after the war ends."

"A good point Brigadier, I'll mention that to him."

Ferguson lights a cigar. "The best thing out of this is that the landing site is secure. Eisenhower can relax now, say what?"

"Right Brigadier, but he still has a hard job ahead."

"A difficult one indeed my boy."

Ferguson puffs on his cigar, then waves it in the air. "Excellent cigars, Cuban, you know. The PM gives them to me. There was a time he didn't have any. That was the time our man Fisher was in his role as Churchill."

"Ha, I remember that Brigadier, The Churchill Equation,"

"A good show that, say what? Let us be off to the club, a brandy is in order. We must celebrate, dear boy."

Two days later, Walker is standing in front of General Eisenhower.

"At ease colonel," Eisenhower said smiling his famous grin.

"You did a fine job colonel, we are all proud of you and how you handle your mission."

"I couldn't have done it without the help of a certain lady, sir."

"Ah, yes Helen Wilkerson. Yes we know all about her, quite a lady."

"Yes she is sir."

"You seem to fancy her, colonel?"

"She is a sweet girl, general."

"Of course she is. Now you may be wondering why I keep calling you colonel instead of lieutenant colonel. The reason is, that you have been promoted to full colonel."

"Thank you sir."

"You earned it son."

Eisenhower spoke into the intercom for Captain Abe to come in.

In a minute, Captain Abe entered with two black boxes in hand.

Eisenhower took one box opened it. "I present you with the Purple Heart for wounds you received in combat."

He pined the medal on Walker's tunic. He took the other box, opened it, and pinned the other medal on the tunic.

"I present you with the Legion Of Merit, for your service to our country."

"Thank you sir."

"You are more than welcome colonel. Now get out of here."

"Yes sir." Walker saluted, did an about face and marched out.

Eisenhower turned to Captain Abe. "Cut some orders, returning him to duty, in command of an engineer regiment."

"Yes sir, right away general." He saluted and marched out.

Eisenhower lit a cigarette, "A good man, that colonel."

EPILOGUE

On June 6, 1944 the invasion begun, the site was the Normandy coast of France.

The original date had been set on June 5, 1944 but was postponed until the next day do to the weather.

Four sites were considered for the landings: Brittany, the Cotentin Peninsula, Normandy, and the Pas de Calais. As Brittany and Cotentin are peninsulas, it would have been possible for the Germans to cut off the Allied advance at a relatively narrow isthmus, so these sites were rejected.

With the Pas de Calais begin the closest point in continental Europe to Britain, the Germans considered it to be the most likely initial landing zone, so it was the most heavily fortified region. But it offered few opportunities for expansion, as the area is bounded by numerous rivers and canals, whereas landings on a broad front in Normandy would permit simultaneous threats against the port of Cherbourg, costal ports further west in Brittany, and an overland attack toward Paris and eventually into Germany. Normandy was hence chosen as the landing site, although the Allies continued to deceive the Germans the attack would come at Pas de Calais.

The target 50-mile stretch of the Normandy coast was divided into five sectors: Utah, Omaha, Gold, Juno and Sword. Utah and Omaha were assigned to American units while Gold and Sword were assigned to British and other allied forces. Juno was assigned to Canadian and other allied forces.

The amphibious landings were preceded by extensive aerial and naval bombardment and an airborne assault, the landing of American, British, and Canadian airborne troops shortly after midnight.

The success of the amphibious landings depended on the establishment of a secure lodgment from which to expand the beachhead to allow the buildup of a well-supplied force capable of breaking out. The amphibious forces were especially vulnerable to strong enemy counter-attacks before the arrival of sufficient forces in the beachhead could be accomplished. To slow or eliminate the enemy's ability to organize and launch counter-attacks during this critical period, airborne operations were used to seize key objectives such as bridges, road crossings, and terrain features, particularly on the eastern and western flanks of the landing areas. The airborne landings some distance behind the beaches were also intended to ease the egress of the amphibious forces off the beaches, and in some cases to neutralize German coastal defense batteries and more quickly expand the area of the beachhead.

The 82nd and 101st Airborne Divisions were assigned to objectives west of Utah Beach, where they hoped to capture and control the few narrow causeways through terrain that had been intentionally flooded by the Germans. Reports from Allied intelligence of the arrival of the German 91st Infantry Division meant the intended drop zones had to be shifted eastward and to the south. The British 6th Airborne Division, on the eastern flank, was assigned to capture intact the bridges over the Caen Canal and River Orne, destroy five bridges over the Dives 6 miles to the east, and destroy the Merville Gun Battery overlooking Sword Beach.

The American airborne landings began with the arrival of pathfinders shortly after midnight. Navigation was difficult because of a bank of thick clouds, and as a result only one of the five paratrooper drop zones was accurately marked with radar signals and Aldis lamps.

Paratroopers from the 101st Airborne were dropped beginning around 01:30, tasked with controlling the causeways behind Utah Beach and destroying road and rail bridges over the Douve River. The C-47s could not fly in a tight formation because of the thick cloud cover, and many paratroopers were dropped far from their intended landing zones. Many planes came in so low that they were under fire from both flak and machine gun fire. Some paratroopers were killed on impact when their parachutes did not have time to open, and others drowned in the flooded fields.

Gathering together into fighting units was made difficult by a shortage of radios and by the bocage terrain, with its hedgerows, stonewalls, and marshes. Some units did not arrive at their targets until afternoon, by which times several of the causeways had already been cleared by members of the 4th Infantry Division moving up from the beach.

Troops of the 82nd Airborne began arriving around 02:30, with the primary objective of capturing two bridges over the River Merderet and destroying two bridges over Douve. On the east side of the river, 75 per cent of the paratroopers landed in or near their drop zone, and within two hours they captured the important crossroads at Sainte-Mere-Eglise and began working to protect the western flank. Because of the pathfinders to accurately mark their drop zone, the two regiments dropped on the west side of the Merderet were extremely scattered, with only four per cent landing in the target area. Many landed in nearby swamps, with much loss of life. Paratroopers consolidated into small groups, usually a combination of men of various ranks from different units, and attempted to concentrate on nearby objectives.

Next came the gliders. Like the paratroopers, many landed far from their drop zones. Even those that landed on target experienced difficulty, with heavy cargo such as Jeeps shifting during landing, crashing through the wooden fuselage, and in some cases crushing personnel on board.

Omaha Beach, the most heavily defended was assigned to the 1st Infantry Division and the 29th Infantry Division. They faced the German 352nd Infantry Division, rather than a single regiment.

Strong currents forced many landing craft east of their intended position of caused them to be delayed. For fear of hitting the landing craft, American bombers delayed releasing their loads and, as a result, most of the beach obstacles at Omaha remained undamaged when the men came ashore. Many of the landing craft ran aground on sandbars and the men had to wade in water up to their necks while under fire to get to the beach.

Utah Beach was in the area defended by two battalions of the 919th Grenadier Regiment. Members of the 8th Infantry Regiment of the 4th Infantry Division were the first to land. Their landing craft were pushed to the south by strong currents, and they found themselves many yards from their intended landing zone. This site turned out to be better, as there was only one strongpoint nearby rather than two, and bombers of IX Bomber Command had bombed the defenses from lower than their prescribed altitude, inflicting considerable damage. In addition, the strong currents had washed ashore many of the underwater obstacles.

On Gold Beach, the first landing was set at a later time due to the differences in the tide between there and the American beaches. High winds made conditions difficult for the landing craft, and the amphibious tanks as they were released close to shore or directly on the beach, instead of further out as planned.

The landing at Juno was delayed because of choppy seas, and the men arrived ahead of their supporting armor, suffering many casualties while disembarking. Most of the offshore bombardment had missed the German defenses. Several exits from the beach were created, but not without difficulty. At Mike beach sector on the western flank, a large crater was filled using an abandoned tank and several rolls of fascine, which were then covered by a temporary bridge. The beach and nearby streets were clogged with traffic for most of the day, making it difficult to move inland.

On Sword Beach, 21 of 25 tanks of the first wave were successful in getting safety ashore to provide cover for the infantry. The beach was heavily mined and peppered with obstacles, making the work of the beach clearing teams difficult and dangerous.

In the windy conditions, tide came in more quickly than expected, so maneuvering the armour was difficult. The beach quickly became congested. Lord Lovat and his 1st Special Service Brigade arrived in the second wave, piped ashore by Private Bill Millin, Lovat's personal piper.

Members of No. 4 Commando moved through Ouistreham to attack from the rear a German gun battery on the shore. Later a concrete observation and control tower at this emplacement was captured.

The Normandy landings were the largest seaborne invasion in history, with nearly 5,000 landing and assault craft. Nearly 160,000 troops crossed the English Channel on D-day. The Allied invasion plans had called for the capture of Carentan, St Lo, Caen, and Bayeux on the first day, with all the beaches linked with a front line 6-10 miles from the beaches; none of these objectives were achieved. The five beachheads were connected on 12 June.

Victory in Normandy stemmed from several factors. German preparations along the Atlantic Wall were only partially finished. The deceptions undertaken by the Allies were successful, leaving the Germans obliged to defend a huge stretch of coastline. The Allies achieved and maintained air supremacy, which meant that the Germans were unable to make observations of the preparations underway in Britain and were unable to interfere via bomber attacks. Infrastructure for transport in France was severely disrupted by Allied bombers and the French Resistance, making it difficult for the Germans to bring up reinforcements and supplies. Some of the opening bombardment was off-target or not concentrated enough to have any impact, but specialized armor worked well except on Omaha, providing close artillery support for the troops as the disembarked onto the other beaches. Indecisiveness and overly complicated command structure on the part of the German high command were also factors in the Allied success.

On 30 April 1945, as the Battle of Berlin raged above him, realizing that all was lost and not wishing to suffer Mussolini's fate, who had been captured and hung, German dictator Adolf Hitler committed suicide in his bunker along with Eva Braun, his long-term partner whom he had married less than 48 hours before their joint suicide.

In his will, Hitler dismissed Reichsmarschall Herman Goring, his second-in-command and Interior Minister Heinrich Himmler after each of them separately tried to seize control of the crumbling Third Reich. Hitler appointed Grossadmiral Karl Donitz as the new Reichsprasident of Germany and Joseph Goebbles as the new Chancellor of Germany. However, Goebbles committed suicide the following day, leaving Donitz as the sole leader of Germany.

The Battle of Berlin ended on 2 May 1945. On that date, General Hekmuth Weidling, the commander of the Berlin Defense Area, unconditionally surrendered the city to General Vasily Chuikov of the Soviet army. On the same day the officers commanding the two armies of Army group Vistula north of Berlin, General Kurt von Tippelskirch, commander of the German 21st Army and General Hasso von Manteuffel, commander of Third Panzer Army, surrendered to the Western Allies.

German forces in North West Germany, Denmark, and the Netherlands surrendered on 4 May 1945. British Field Marshal Bernard Montgomery took the unconditional military surrender at Luncberg from Generaladmiral Hans-Georg von Friedburg, and General Eberhard Kinzel, of all German forces in Holland, in northwest Germany including the Frisian Islands and Heligoland and all other islands, in Schleswig-Holstein, and in Denmark, including all naval ships in these areas.

On 5 May, Grossadmiral Donitz ordered all U-boats to cease offensive operations and return to their bases.

On 6 May, Reichsmarshall and Hitler's second in command, Herman Goring, surrendered to General Carl Spaatz, who was the commander of the operational United States Air Forces in Europe, along with his wife and daughter at the German-Austria border.

General Alfred Jodl arrived in Reims, France and, following Donitz's instructions, offered to surrender all forces fighting the Western Allies. This was exactly the same negotiating position that von Friedeburg had initially made to Montgomery, and like Montgomery, the Supreme Allied Commander, General Eisenhower threatened to break off all negotiations unless the Germans agreed to a complete unconditional surrender to all the Allies on all fronts. Eisenhower explicitly told Jodl that he would order western lines closed to German soldiers, thus forcing them to surrender to the Soviets. Jodl sent a signal to Donitz informing him of Eisenhower's declaration. Shortly after midnight, Donitz, accepting the inevitable, sent a signal to Jodl authorizing the complete total surrender of all German forces.

In the early morning hours of 7 May at headquarters in Reims France, the Chief-of-Staff of the German Armed Forces High Command, General Alfred Jodl, signed an unconditional surrender documents for all German forces to the Allies. All German forces were to cease active operations effective the next day, 8 May 1945.

Wilhelm Keitel and other German High Command representatives traveled to Berlin, and shortly before midnight signed an amended and definitive document of unconditional surrender, explicitly surrendering to all the Allied forces in the presence of Marshal Georgi Zhukov.

German forces on the Channel Islands except for Aldenery surrendered on 8 May after they were informed by the German authorities that the war was over.

News of the imminent surrender broke in the west on 8 May, and celebrations erupted throughout Europe and the British Empire.

Although the military commanders of most German forces obeyed the order of surrender issued by the German Armed Forces High Command, not all commanders did so. The largest contingent were Army Group Centre under the command of Generalfeldmarschall Ferdinand Schorner who had been promoted to Commander-in-Chief of the Army on 30 April in Hitler's last will and testament. On 8 May, Schorner deserted his command and flew to Austria; the Soviet Army sent overwhelming forces against Army Group Centre in the Prague Offensive, forcing German units in Army Group Centre to capitulate by 11 May.

On 13 May, the Red Army halted all offensives in Europe. Isolated pockets of resistance in Czechoslovakia were mopped up by this date.

The garrison on Alderney Island surrendered on 16 May, one week after the garrison on the other Channel Islands, Guernsey and Jersey surrendered.

The Georgian Uprising of Texel was Europe's last battlefield in World War II. It was fought between Georgian Nazi-collaborationist army units on Texel against the German occupiers of that Dutch island. This battle ended on 20 May.

Karl Donitz continued to act as if he were the German head of state, but his Flensburg government, so called because it was based at Flensburg in northern Germany and controlled only a small area around the town, was not recognized by the Allies. On 12 May an Allied liaison team arrived in Flensburg and took quarters aboard the passenger ship Patria. The liaison officers and the Supreme Allied Headquarters soon realized that they had no need to act through the Flensburg government and that its members should be arrested. On 23 May, acting on Allied Headquarters orders and with the approval of the Soviets, American Major General Rooks summoned Donitz aboard the

Patria and communicated to him that he and all the members of his government were under arrest, and that their government was dissolved.

Four weeks after the war ended, Colonel Walker was ordered to appear at General Eisenhower's Headquarters. He arrives in his best uniform and reports to Captain Abe.

"Wait here, Colonel," said Abe. He knocked on Eisenhower's door and entered."

"Colonel Walker is here sir."

"Good, show him in captain."

Abe turned and opened the door. "Come in colonel."

Walker marched in and saluted, standing ramrod straight.

Eisenhower smiled, returned the salute, "At ease colonel."

Eisenhower stood and picked up a black box from his desk.

He came around from the desk and stood in front of Walker.

He opened the box, took the medal from the box and pinned it on Walker's tunic. "I present you with the Distinguish Service Cross for you actions on Omaha Beach. You did a hell of a good job out there colonel, leading your engineer regiment under heavy five. Your men saved many of our boys clearing mines so they could move inland."

"Thank you sir."

"Thank you, colonel, without you and your men, we may have had a very difficult time getting off the beach. I am sure many of your men deserve decorations."

"Yes sir, I have already taken care of that."

"Very well then. I see you are due to rotate back to the States soon."

"Yes sir, I have been notified of that."

"I have issued orders for a 30 day leave for you to take either here or in the States, which ever you like is up to you."

"That sounds nice sir."

"Well, you deserve it colonel. Will you take it stateside or here?"

"Actually sir, I believe Alderney Island is nice this time of year."

Eisenhower smiled his famous smile. "You're dismissed colonel."

Walked saluted smartly, did an about face and marched out the door.